Becoming Desperate

Book One

in the Desperate Horse Wives Trilogy

Janet R Fox

ISBN-10: 1976435722
ISBN-13:978-1976435720

To Pam,
Happy trails to you!
Janet R Fox

DEDICATION

To the volunteers of the Last Chance Corral who
are dedicated to saving the nurse mare foals,
To the many volunteers who help make Equine
Affaire possible each year,
And as always, to Jack, my hero,
And Dave, my brother

CONTENTS

1 Elise 1

2 Lavern 46

3 Bristol 88

4 Nancy 134

5 Desperate Horse Wives 169

ACKNOWLEDGMENTS

Thank you to my dear friend Judy Moyer for the use of the photograph for the cover of this book. She is riding her horse Scooter.

1 ELISE

Elise Evans made it to her junior year in high school without losing her virginity.

She had a few boyfriends off and on since eighth grade, but in junior high, there had been no opportunity for extended privacy. Now in high school and finally allowed to date, she had not been that enthralled with the boys who asked her out.

Marty Parker was different. He was more outgoing and personable than the others, and he seemed more exciting and worldly to her. He had the upper classman mystic. He drove a brand-new Corvette. He always knew the answers in the third period Political Science 101 class the University of Akron offered juniors and seniors for college credit. Even the professor who taught the class seemed to respect him for his ideas shared in class discussions. Marty was the editor of the school newspaper, as big a man on campus as he could be without being a football or basketball star.

As well as being together third period, Marty and Elise both spent fifth period in Miss Herman's classroom working on projects for the paper. However, he never seemed to notice her. Elise felt that her plain face and limp, brown hair would never attract

Marty's attention. True, Marty was not handsome, just average looking, but he was so, well, so worldly and sophisticated. She hoped she could capture his interest with her intelligence and her plans of becoming a lawyer.

Now, as they worked on the paper together, laying out the columns and the ads to fit the format, she told him she wanted to be a family lawyer. "I know there're kids in foster care who need a committed advocate, and old people who need protection from their family members who want to take away their rights just so they can grab their money. I really want a career that will allow me to accomplish some good in this world."

Marty made no comment. Elise rambled on, "I thought about being a criminal prosecutor, but I don't think I could argue for the death penalty. What if the person really was innocent, you know? Look at all the people who are finally set free after years in prison when DNA proves their innocence. What if they had been put to death first for something they hadn't done? You can't fix that."

"I think the football schedule will fit here. Hand it to me," he instructed, ignoring her rambling.

"If they are guilty, they really do deserve it, you know?" Elise said, handing Marty the schedule. "I mean, if they killed innocent people, like if they tortured them, hurt children, murdered a whole family, you know? But should we play God? Do we have the right to do to them what they did? But the biggest thing, you know, is what if they didn't do it, and we think they did, I mean the jury thinks so? If they were just in prison instead of dead, we could at least let them out of prison if we find out they didn't do it."

"So, I think being a family lawyer is what I want to do. I could be helpful to a lot of people who would otherwise be in some trouble." Elise looked at Marty who was looking at the computer screen, ignoring her.

Elise's back was hurting from bending over the work table. She straightened, put her hands on her hips, and bent backward from her waist to stretch in the other direction. Unwittingly, it thrust her breasts into her shirt front, outlining her lace camisole and her nipples through the thin, white, cotton material.

Marty was looking now, not at her face, but at her well-rounded twin peaks. "Um, do you have a date for the football game this weekend?"

Elise, shocked, popped back to straight vertical. "What?" She was too speechless to give him an answer. *Is he asking me out? Or does he just wonder if I'm dating someone? I don't want him to think I'm not dating anyone, but what do I say?*

"Well, do you want to go with me or not?" Marty asked indifferently. "Eddie, our sports writer, will be out of town with his family this weekend. I'm covering the game for the paper. If you want to go, I'll pick you up at six-thirty."

"Oh. Well, yeah, I mean, yes, I'll go. Want me to help you write the story?"

Without answering her, Marty asked for her address, directions to her house, and her phone number in case something came up to change the plans. When the bell rang, he did not offer to walk her to her next class.

Elise spent the rest of the week worrying that something would come up to cancel the date, and wondering why Marty did not talk to her at school. True, there was no opportunity during third period, and each day Miss Herman had stayed in her room to grade papers during fifth period, but he could have made an effort before or after class. She was excited about the possible date, but disappointed in his lack of attention. While she was apprehensive about his indifference, Elise gave him the excuse that he was a private person. She hoped that he would open up and talk with her more when they were out together. Despite her concerns, she daydreamed about Marty asking her to go steady and driving her to and from school in his sports car.

Maybe he would take her to the Lujan's drive-in in neighboring Tallmadge. All the cool kids went there. The ones with the coolest cars showed off by circling the restaurant two or three times before pulling into a parking slot. Surely Marty's shiny, new Vette deserved three times around. She would feel so honored! *I hope the kids from our school will be there that night to see me in his car with him.*

The homecoming dance was coming up, and if all went well, maybe he would ask her to go. *Oh, my gosh, I'll have to get a dress and shoes to go with it.*

When the bell rang to end fifth period on Friday, Marty nonchalantly reminded her, "See you at six-thirty," grabbed his books, and hurried out the door.

Thrilled, Elise stood there with mouth open, watching him leave. *He's taking me tonight! It's happening!*

She drifted through the rest of the school day in a hazy mind fog. Luckily, the teachers had not called on her in her last classes, and they gave no tests. The final bell energized her, and she hurried home to plan for her date. She had to try to do something with her hair and to make her final choice on what to wear to the game. That turned out to be her tightest pair of boot-cut blue jeans, which were not tight enough to make her father complain, and a sweater set that hugged her curves. She would carry a lap blanket for later when the chill of an early fall evening would settle in. It would be fun to cuddle with Marty under its warmth.

Her brother lived in the dorm at Kent State University and would not be home. Both of her parents worked and would not be home until close to six. They insisted on eating dinner together as a family as much as possible, so Elise was going to cook. She asked them to come straight home from work. She wanted to have dinner on the table right at six o'clock so that she could be ready in time for Marty. They agreed.

Everything worked out well except for her hair. She ended up pulling it back into a pony tail. Her sweater set gave her a soft, feminine appearance. She had dinner ready when her parents came home, and they had finished eating before Marty arrived. There was just enough time to brush her teeth, apply a little lipstick, and squirt a dash of her mother's perfume on her neck and wrists. *Should I open the door when he comes, or should I be upstairs and make him wait on me for a couple of minutes?*

Elise opted to answer the door herself and introduce him to her parents. That would seem more sophisticated than seeming to be running late and leaving the three of them to introduce themselves. *I hope he parks and comes to the door. Dad won't let me go out with him if he doesn't come in to get me.*

Marty did come to the door for her. Elise let him in with a smile. Her parents were sitting on the couch. They stood and she introduced them. "Mom, Dad, this is Marty Parker. Marty, these are my parents, Mr. and Mrs. Evans."

"Nice to meet you," he told them as they shook hands.

"Nice to meet you, too, Marty. You take good care of our girl, and have her home by eleven-thirty, hear?" her father told him.

"Yes, sir. We have to go now to make the game on time." Marty took her elbow and guided her toward the door. Elise thrilled at his touch.

She grabbed her purse and the lap blanket on their way out. Marty noticed it and smiled. He had brought one, too. He helped Elise into his Corvette, and for the benefit of her parents, he drove off sedately.

Neither of them spoke for the first two miles. Although she was nervous, Elise was too keyed up to stay silent for long. "This is a really nice car." *A really cool car, but it sure rides rough.*

"Uh, huh. It's an early graduation gift from my folks."

"Wow. It seems more like a college grad gift than for high school. You're really lucky. After paying for my college, I doubt my parents will buy me any kind of a car. But after I'm a practicing attorney, I can pay them back for my education and buy myself a nice car. Where are you going to go to school? What are you going to do?"

Marty glanced at Elise quickly, then returned his eyes to the road. "To Xavier University in Cincinnati, general studies until I decide on a major." He placed his hand on her knee.

Elise's heart fluttered. She wanted to touch him back, but she was afraid to. *I can't believe I'm on a date with Marty Parker! I wonder if he'll kiss me when he takes me home.*

"You don't have any brothers or sisters, do you Marty?" With difficulty, she controlled her voice to keep her excitement from showing.

He glanced at her again. "Yeah, I have two brothers, both grown and married. They both have kids, so I'm an uncle. I was a surprise baby."

"So, you're Uncle Marty! Huh!" The thought of that made him seem even older and wiser to her. "I bet you've changed some diapers."

"Nope, I don't want anything to do with those. I don't babysit."

Elise wondered whether she would be meeting his family soon. She was both terrified and eager to meet them. She hoped they would like and accept her.

They arrived at the football field. They waved at friends and spoke briefly with those close to them. Elise felt proud to be seen with Marty. During the first half of the game, Marty paid little attention to her. He was busy taking notes for the school paper on the action happening on the field. During half time, he excused himself and talked with several of his buddies. They stood around joking and laughing while Elise sat alone as the school bands performed. She wondered why Marty could be so personable with others while disregarding her.

During the third quarter, Marty became more attentive. The crisp fall evening began to chill. He tucked a blanket around her without asking if she was cold. He leaned into her and reached for her hand under the blanket. Elise was thrilled. *Finally,* she thought.

When he pulled his hand away to take more notes, she snuggled against him. During the next time-out on the field, he slipped his hand back under the blanket, but this time he put his arm around her and pulled her close. When she snuggled contentedly, he tentatively touched her breast with his finger tips. Startled, she stiffened, but did not pull away. At first, she was nervous, concerned that she should not allow him to touch her this way. By the fourth quarter, hidden by the blanket, he was massaging her nipples in small circles and caressing her breasts as she relaxed against him, no longer watching the game, no longer apprehensive.

When the game ended, he stood, and without offering his hand to help her up, commanded, “Come on, let’s go.” Without looking back, he started down the bleachers.

“Where? Where are we going?” Elise hoped he was taking her to Lujan’s, but he did not answer. He was hurrying through the crowd, and she had trouble keeping up with him. As eager as she was to be his girlfriend, his lack of attention made her uneasy.

He drove them to an oil well down a dirt lane off a country road. Elise did not know whether she was thrilled or worried. He had not talked to her during the drive, and she was too confused to try to begin a conversation. *Maybe I shouldn't have let him touch me that way.*

"Marty, what time is it? You know I have to be home by eleven-thirty. What are you doing? Where are we going?" Elise clasped her elbows and hugged her arms to her chest. The evening was not going as she had dreamed.

"We're here," he told her. Marty shut off the engine and turned to her. "This is a bit difficult in a sports car, but we can manage."

"Manage what?" Instead of answering her, he unbuckled both of their seat belts, and opened his door to go around to her side of the car. He opened her door and pulled her out of the low-slung seat.

"Here, I'll sit down, and you sit on my lap." Marty managed to maneuver Elise into straddling him in the tight quarters. "If this doesn't work, we can spread the blankets on the ground."

Marty's tentative kisses became more intense as his hand lifted Elise's shirt and fumbled with her bra hooks. She knew she should stop him, but it felt too good. *Maybe in a few more minutes.*

Marty groaned as his hands unhooked her bra and found her breasts. "Is this OK? If you want me to stop, you have to say no, but say it now, because in a minute I won't be able to stop."

Her body responded to his words with a thrill she had never before experienced. *He really knows what he's doing. He's so sophisticated and experienced, but he chooses me!*

While she was edgy about allowing him to caress her under her clothes, she was enjoying these strange, new sensations. *It feels so good!*

As his hands flicked and brushed and kneaded, she answered him with a sigh that turned into a soft groan of her own.

…

During October, Marty picked up Elise on Friday nights. They went to the football home games, ending up at the oil well each time. If it was an away-game night, they drove directly to the oil well. When Marty discovered that Elise was a virgin, he began to bring condoms with him. "Until you get yourself on the pill," he told her. "I don't like wearing these."

Marty still tended to ignore her at school. When there was time before her eleven-thirty curfew, he did take her to Lujan's after satisfying himself at the oil well. He always made three complete circles of the parking lot before sliding into a parking place to order a couple of colas. Elise was proud to be seen with Marty in his Corvette, but she felt uneasy about their relationship. It did not seem to her that he was in love with her, not even close. She began to realize that she did not know exactly what love was, and she questioned whether she loved him.

On the first Friday night in November as they circled the drive-in, the kids in the parked cars began laughing and pointing at them. Marty parked and ordered their colas through the speaker. When the waitress delivered them to the driver's side door, she snickered. "What have you two been up to?" she asked coyly as she pointed to the bottom of his door.

“What?” Marty was confused. He handed both drinks to Elise, then stepped out of the car. When his door opened, it freed his used condom, which promptly fell onto the pavement. It had been caught in his door, flapping in the breeze as they drove down the road and circled the parking lot. Marty snorted and kicked it under his car. He said nothing to Elise as he climbed back in and took his drink from her.

“What was it? Why were they laughing?”

He sipped his coke. “Nothing. Don’t worry about it.”

Marty did not tell her, but on Monday she found out from two of her friends at school just before sixth period. The other students had been giving her strange glances all day. Some of them whispered and snickered together when they saw her. Now Elise knew why. She was so embarrassed she spent the rest of the school day in the clinic.

Tuesday morning, she told her mother that she thought she might throw up. This was true. She had not been able to eat dinner the night before, and she could not sleep all night. Her mother told her she could stay home from school. Elise put the covers over her head as though to hide from the world. When her parents both left for work, she cried until she had no more tears. She had lost her virginity, her reputation, and her dignity, but for what? *He doesn’t love me, and I don’t love him!*

Upon reaching that realization, Elise decided to break up with Marty. She was in way over her head with him. She decided that the longer she stayed out of school, the more attention she would draw to herself. She would have to go back tomorrow, try to hold her head up, and let this blow over. Eventually, everyone would forget. *Right, easier said than done.* She cried huge, dry sobs.

On Wednesday, it did seem that the incident had been forgotten. There was plenty of other gossip. Three girls were in a fight in the restroom during home room. First period, a kid broke his ankle during gym class, and Todd and Krista, the homecoming king and queen, broke up. During second period, Tommy Barns was caught throwing Vanessa James' small purse down the tuba in the band room. No one could shake it out. Best of all, the Spanish teacher, Mr. Banks, had his zipper down during all of second period.

Elise was going to tell Marty during fifth period that she did not want to go out with him again, but three other students were there working on the school paper. As usual, Marty ignored her. On Friday, when the bell rang to end fifth period, he grabbed his books and tossed, "See you at six-thirty," over his shoulder.

Elise stopped him before he could walk away. "Uh, Marty, I'm not going. I can't do this anymore."

He stopped in his tracks and gave her a long, appraising look. "Well, it was good while it lasted. It's too cold now to go back to the oil well anyway. Thanks, Toots." He shrugged and dashed out the door. She followed in time to see him catch up to Krista, put his arm around her waist, then walk her down the hall.

Breaking up with Marty was a relief, but that feeling did not last long.

When her brother, Wyatt, came home from Kent State for the Thanksgiving weekend, he knocked on Elise's bedroom door. He had the same brown hair and green eyes as his sister, but he had the long eye lashes that Elise had always thought should have been hers.

"Hey, little sister. I hear you've been down in the dumps since you stopped dating Marty. What's up? Did he mean that much to you?" Wyatt sat on the floor in front of her bed. Elise was sitting on her bed with her math homework on her lap.

"Oh, no, not really. Didn't Mom tell you that I was the one who broke up with him?" She used the pencil eraser to brush a stray hair from her cheek.

"Yeah, she mentioned that, but she also told me you seem preoccupied or something. What's up?"

Elise shrugged. "Just school, homework, you know."

"OK, then. But you know, I've been amiss as your big brother not to have had a talk with you about dating boys before you actually started to, so I'm glad you didn't see that Marty guy for very long. Look, I just want you to know that, well, that you need to be careful. Lots of boys only want what they can get. Just be careful and don't get carried away. Don't trust them with, with, well, just don't give it away. Know what I mean?"

Elise burst into tears. "It's already too late. I think I'm pregnant."

...

Elise's periods had always been irregular, but now she was worried because she had not had a period since before she had gone out with Marty. She had not worried about pregnancy because, except for the first two times, he had used condoms, but she had never gone this long between periods before.

She begged Wyatt not to tell their parents. "I don't know what to do, but I don't want them to know!"

"Well, little sister, you sure laid one on me. I have to get my head wrapped around this. Just know that I love you no matter what. OK, oh, man, umm, yes, no, we won't tell Mom and Dad for now. Maybe you aren't even pregnant. We'll make sure first. So, you're not on the pill? Did he use protection?"

"Yes, Marty did. So maybe I'm not pregnant."

~~Marty~~ Wyatt reached up from his seat on the floor by her bed to touch her arm. "I hate to tell you, but that isn't always one hundred percent sure. Those things can break or leak or something. And did he use something every time? How far along are you, I mean, if you are."

"I don't know. I really don't know." Embarrassed and miserable, Elise hid her face with her long hair and sobbed quietly.

"OK, pull yourself together, or our folks will know something's wrong. Try not to worry. I'll be here for you. What about Marty? Does he know there's a chance you're pregnant?"

"No. We don't even talk anymore. He ignores me like I don't exist. I wouldn't want to tell him, either, unless I knew for sure." Elise pounded her pillow in frustration.

"OK, OK." Wyatt stood up and sat on the edge of her bed. He took her hand in his. "The first thing we have to do is to find out if you are pregnant. If you aren't, then great, but you have to tell Mom that you need to see a doctor to find out why you aren't, you know, having your periods."

Elise pulled her hand away and hugged her pillow to her chest. "And if I am? What then?"

"Then you have to tell Mom and start to see a doctor anyway, for that. And Marty would have to be told. I mean, he should take some responsibility here, but let's not worry that far ahead for now. I'll get to a drug store as soon as I can while I'm home this weekend and pick up a test kit for you. That's the first step, to find out if you are or aren't pregnant. If you are, we'll deal with it together, you, me, Mom and Dad, and I would hope, Marty."

Wyatt stood up, patted the top of his sister's head, and bent to kiss her forehead. "I promise it will all work out."

…

When Rose Evans asked Wyatt to run to the store for the dinner rolls she had forgotten to buy, he had his chance to pick up the pregnancy test kit. Hoping to save the family's early afternoon Thanksgiving dinner from being spoiled, he did not slip the test to Elise until early in the evening.

Elise immediately locked herself in the upstairs bathroom to use it. She followed the directions and waited for the longest three minutes of her life. When the reading appeared on the test stick, her knees gave way and she folded to the floor. She clung to the side of the bath tub and stared at the stick in her hand. She was too shocked for tears.

When Wyatt gently knocked on the bathroom door, Elise grabbed the test stick and directions, stuffed them in the box, and quickly wrapped it in toilet paper and stuck it in the waste basket. "Yeah, I'm coming. Just a sec," she croaked from vocal chords that were constricted with fear. She added more tissue on top to hide the evidence better, washed her hands, and opened the door.

Wyatt glimpsed his sister's stricken expression just as she threw her arms around him and buried her face into his chest. He held her for a minute before advising her, "We need to tell Mom and Dad. Let's do it now and get it over with. I'll be with you. We all love you. It'll be OK. This isn't anything you're going to be doing alone. Come on."

Elise could barely walk down the stairs on her shaking legs. She had one hand on the railing and one on Wyatt's shoulder ahead of her. She staggered into the living room in a trance. Their mother registered the concern on her son's face and the zombie-like look on her daughter's, jumped up from her easy chair, and rushed to her children. "Joe!" she called for her husband. "What is it? What's the matter? What's wrong?" she asked her children.

Joe Evans hurried into the room in time to see his daughter grab his wife and hang on.

"I'm sorry, I'm sorry. I'm so sorry," Elise sobbed repeatedly as she held her mother tight.

Rose smoothed her daughter's hair, shushed her, and cooed to her to soothe her as she looked worriedly at her son.

"What's going on here?" Joe asked of all of them.

Elise did not seem capable of explaining, so Wyatt told them, "Everything's going to be all right. We just have some things to work out. Elise is pregnant."

Elise was now crying hysterically. Rose continued to shush and coo while trying to process Wyatt's announcement. Joe folded his tall frame onto his chair with a heavy sigh and put his head in his hands. Wyatt grabbed the box of tissues and handed them to his mother, who had guided Elise to the couch. She handed a wad of tissues to her daughter. No one spoke until Elise quieted to the occasional hiccupy sob.

"Obviously, we have many questions." Joe was crestfallen. "Tell us what you can. You're still my princess." Knowing that his daughter was traumatized, Joe was making an effort to hide his disappointment.

Elise sobbed out the bare bones of her story, punctuated with many an, "I'm so sorry." Her family listened without interrupting. Rose stroked her hair, Wyatt sat on the floor in front of the couch holding her hand, and Joe sat with his hand held thoughtfully over his mouth and chin, elbow on the arm of his chair.

"What am I going to do now?" Elise wailed when she had told them all that she could.

Joe, a practical man, began to formulate a plan. "You need to finish your high school education, no matter what."

"But I want to go to college, too, and study law," she moaned.

Joe removed his hand from his face and gripped the arms of his chair. "When we make choices, we are choosing one thing over another and that often means a sacrifice of the other thing. This thing will not be easy, but we will deal with it as a family."

Rose and Wyatt nodded in agreement. Elise blew her nose.

Joe continued, "You're smart enough to earn your GED, probably in less than the two years it would take you to finish high school. You'll want to look into that program before you start showing, assuming you want to avoid embarrassment in front of your classmates. Marty and his family need to know as soon as possible. They should be involved in this. Will he marry you? Do you want to marry him? Good grief, you're so young! Either way, he needs to be responsible for some support. We need to be thinking of what's best for this baby as well as for yourself."

"I don't know. I don't know what I want," Elise whispered. "I just want to be a family lawyer."

Joe rubbed his brow. "That may or may not happen now. But that's long term. We need to think more short term right now."

"Yeah, like what to name the baby." Wyatt tried to joke to lighten the mood, but no one laughed. "Hey, we are keeping this baby, aren't we? I mean, that's not up for debate, is it?"

They all looked at each other in shock, but no one could speak until Wyatt followed up with, "I don't necessarily mean abortion. I mean, there is the adoption option."

"What, give away my own grandchild? I think not." Rose was adamant. "And of course, we cannot kill our baby."

"But doesn't that depend on how far along she is?" Joe asked. "If it's just an embryo, just some cells?"

Humiliated and ashamed, Elise felt that her opinion did not count. Her mother answered. "I don't know. Maybe I could give some thought to abortion during the first two months when it's an embryo and not yet a baby. But I think I would still feel like we were killing our grandchild."

"Well, Rose, get her a doctor appointment and let's go from there," Joe told his wife. "After that, we can decide what to say to the Parkers. But one thing's certain, young lady, you are to finish your high school education even if you have to live at home and have some help with this baby. Rose, make that doctor appointment." Dejected and heavy with this burden, he heaved himself from the chair and went upstairs to bed without saying good-night.

...

It was the end of the second week in December when the busy gynecologist had an opening and Rose could make the appointment. The doctor determined that Elise was about eight weeks pregnant.

Dr. Julie Kennedy had made Elise as comfortable as possible during the exam. She asked questions and provided information in a non-judgmental manner. "I don't know how much thought you have given your options here," she told Rose and Elise, her brown eyes looking at each of them in turn. "I can recommend legitimate adoption agencies. They would provide counseling to help you be sure of your decision to adopt."

Dr. Julie, as she asked to be called, smoothed a lock of her short blond hair from her forehead and continued. "Of course, abortion is another option. If that is your choice, I would recommend that procedure being done within the next week because you are already at eight weeks. At ten weeks, the fetus feels pain. I don't know if you know how the little one is aborted? What happens during an abortion?"

Rose and Elise both shook their head no. The doctor continued. "The fetus is vacuumed out of the womb. It often tears the body of the little one apart. Ultrasounds show the baby trying to swim away from the reach of the vacuum."

Rose and Elise both looked horrified. Dr. Julie continued, "I know. It is horrible. I hate to be this graphic, but you need all the facts to make an informed decision. I strongly feel that if you are making a decision for the best interest of this baby as well as for yourself, and you decide that means abortion, then you should carry out the termination within a week. Of course, it is still legal after nine weeks, but…" Dr. Julie let the weight of her description linger. She tapped her clipboard twice with her ink pen.

Elise clutched her chest and cried out, "I can't do that to my baby!"

Rose reasoned, "Well, maybe now, within this week before there's a beating heart and before it feels any pain. Maybe that would be best for you and the baby. I mean, you can't really support a baby and get your education. I mean, we would try to help all we could, but there's only so much…"

Dr. Julie shook her head no and cut in. "I'm afraid it's already too late. Your baby has had a beating heart since it was eighteen days old. At twenty-eight days she had eyes, ears, a tongue, and tiny budding legs and arms. Of course, now, at fifty-six days or so, those little legs and arms are much longer and she has a steady heart beat. It will be twelve more weeks until you feel them, but your baby is making body movements now. She has a skeleton, and her brain is coordinating the movement of her muscles and organs. Yes, brain waves can be detected at forty-two days! Honey, this is why I'm asking you to carefully consider what it means to abort. This is a baby, not a collection of cells. At eight or nine weeks, we stop calling her an embryo and call her a fetus, meaning little one."

"You know the sex of my baby?" Elise asked Dr. Julie. "She's a girl? I'm having a girl?"

"No, it's too early to tell the gender of your baby, but I can tell you in another two or three months."

The doctor tapped her clipboard again. "Another option for you, if you decide to keep your baby, is to seek help from one of the pregnancy care agencies. There are two in Summit County and one in Portage county. These are non-judgmental agencies with the purpose of helping low income mothers keep and support their babies. They give diapers, baby formula, clothing, cribs, and other items, as they have them available. I think they offer parenting classes, too. You know, these babies don't come with instructions."

"Tell you what. I'm sure you need some time to discuss this. I'll have the receptionist give you a pamphlet on the developmental stages of the fetus and some from the pregnancy care agencies. Just don't take too long to decide about termination. Any questions?"

Rose's mouth had dropped open. Elise's eyes were wide. Neither one answered, so the doctor tapped her clipboard one more time and walked out.

"Well, I had no idea!" Rose exclaimed. "I think we're having a baby."

"Yeah, Mom. We are definitely having this baby. There is no way we are doing that to her. Did you hear? She already has brain waves and a beating heart!" Elise hugged her belly, trying to cuddle her baby. For the first time since discovering she was pregnant, she smiled.

...

Joe Evans agreed the pregnancy should not be terminated, or, in Elise's words, that her baby not be killed. Elise called Wyatt to tell him she was definitely keeping the baby. He came home for a family meeting that weekend.

"Uncle Wyatt's home!" he announced, coming in the door. He gave his sister and mother each a hug and slapped his father on the back.

Dinner was not a strained affair as the news of the baby had finally sunk in and become an accepted reality. Elise was relieved to have her secret out in the open and to have her family's support. She did not care either way whether Marty Parker would become involved.

After dinner, the family moved to the living room to discuss the upcoming meeting with the Parkers. Her father spoke first. "The Parkers may have guessed what this meeting is about even though I refused to say so when I set it up. Why else would we have requested it? There are two outcomes I think we should attempt. One is to have Marty give this baby legitimacy, the other is to have his financial support, or that of his parents, until the time when he is gainfully employed, whether or not he marries Elise."

Elise sat at the other end of the couch from her mother. "I don't care if he doesn't want to marry me. I really don't like him much anymore."

"Oh, dear." Rose sniffed and reached for the box of tissues.

"Well, you liked him well enough to ..." Joe stopped himself by clearing his throat. "So, um, let's begin, of course, with the fact that Elise is pregnant, and that the baby is Marty's doing. We'll give them some time to deal with the shock factor, then explain that we want our daughter to finish her schooling, and suggest that Marty do the same. He's a senior, so that won't be difficult. Then we'll ask when they feel the best time for a wedding would be. Preferably, we should schedule a wedding before she's showing, although people will guess why a sixteen-year-old is getting married. Obviously, it will be a simple civil ceremony." Joe looked at his wife and daughter on the couch, and at his son seated on the floor in front of Elise.

"And if Marty refuses to marry her?" Wyatt asked.

"I won't care," Elise reminded them, as she reached for the tissues and blotted her eyes.

Joe answered, "If Marty refuses to marry her, we then bring up child support and try to arrive at an agreement as to an amount. We will attempt to keep it out of the courts, but we will have our agreement drawn up by a lawyer for both parties to sign."

The family meeting ended ten minutes later. Elise dreaded the Sunday afternoon meeting with the Parkers. The one with her own loving family was ordeal enough. She felt that her father was pushing for a marriage she was not sure about. It would be respectable to give her baby the father's last name, to be sure of child support, and to have the father involved in raising the baby. Elise felt strongly that it is always sad for children not to have a father involved in their life.

...

The Sunday meeting with the Parkers was even more uncomfortable than Elise feared. The Parker family reception of the Evans family was not cordial. Marty's two older brothers, Andy and Sean, were there along with Marty, his father Devon, and his mother Alice. The entire Evans family had arrived together, Joe, Rose, Wyatt, and Elise.

After introductions were made and everyone was seated, Mr. Parker asked without tact, "So, why are you here?"

There had been no offers of refreshments, no smiles, no welcoming greetings.

Joe took the lead from Devon Parker and moved right down to business. He leaned forward in his chair. "Well, Devon, we have …"

Devon interrupted him with a correction. "Mr. Parker," he admonished Joe.

"Sorry, Mr. Parker, then. So, we have a mutual problem."

As he was about to explain, Devon interrupted again. "Oh, I doubt that any problem of yours is mutual."

Joe sat back in his chair. It was all he could do to control his temper. He did lose his patience with attempting to be tactful, and he blurted out, "It *is* a problem for you when your son has made my daughter pregnant."

Devon tipped his head back and roared. Marty looked at his father and began laughing, too.

Joe stood up with clenched fists. Wyatt quickly stood by his father's side and gently led him back to his seat by his arm.

The laughter ended. Devon remained seated. He spoke first. "So, now you want to punch me out after insulting my son by accusing him of making your daughter pregnant? I don't even know if she is pregnant, or if she is, whose it is."

Joe's fist gripped the arms of the chair tightly and his jaw clenched. Wyatt glared at the man. It was Elise who spoke up. "We know because the doctor confirmed it. I'm nine weeks pregnant, which means the baby is nine weeks old, has a heartbeat and brain waves, and Marty knows she's his because I was a virgin when he touched me, and I haven't been with anyone else." Elise's face was red with the effort of confronting the Parkers and from the embarrassment of her situation; however, she was proud of advocating for herself.

"Is this true, son?" Devon asked.

"Dad, I don't know if she's pregnant. Yeah, she was a virgin when I was with her, but she broke up with me. For all I know, it was to be with some other guy. Who knows how many guys she was with after me?" Marty smirked.

"No one. No one but you," Elise whispered, as Wyatt jumped up with every intention of punching Marty.

Joe grabbed his son and held him back. "Look. Elise is pregnant. She was a virgin until your son, when your son, when they were together," he sputtered. "She has not been with anyone else. Now she's pregnant. Now we're here to make a plan for how to handle the situation. We expect you to be civil about this. We thought that since the baby is also at least half Marty's responsibility, you would want to participate in this planning." Joe gently pushed Wyatt back into his seat and sat back down in his own chair.

"If it's a matter of needing money to pay for an abortion, I believe we can help there, even not knowing whose baby it is. After all, my son did acknowledge that he was with her."

Joe was adamant. "No, no abortion. This is our grandchild and your grandchild, too. Abortion is not an option for our family."

"I don't understand. Why not terminate the problem? Then everyone can finish school and go on with their lives, no more problem. Devon said we will pay for it." This was the first time that Alice Parker contributed to the conversation.

"I repeat, not an option."

Andy spoke up, only half in jest. Knowing that the Parkers in the room outnumbered the Evans, he suggested, "Let's take a vote." He and Marty smirked and fist bumped.

Elise held her arms against her stomach. "She's not an embryo, not an it. OK, maybe she is a problem, but she's a problem to be planned for, not a problem to be voted on, terminated, or eliminated. She's a baby, my baby, and I won't kill her."

"Well, I hardly think you're old enough to make your own decisions," Alice snapped.

Rose moved over to sit closer to her daughter. "Oh, the Evans family all agree with her. Well said, my girl." Rose reached out, touched Elise's arm, and smiled at her.

Devon continued to argue for abortion, but the Evans were unwavering on that point. "What do you suggest? Surely, you aren't proposing perpetual child support? We'll pay for an abortion, but that's it. We won't allow you to extort us!"

Joe explained, "We aren't interested in extortion, only in having Marty take his share of responsibility. Yes, that would mean child support, but we would expect that you, his family, would share in that while he finishes school. We expect Elise to finish by earning a GED. If you're interested in being part of this baby's life, and, after all, she is your flesh and blood, then I suggest that a marriage is appropriate. It would be in the baby's best interest to have two parents and two sets of grandparents. We can pursue child support legally, but we can also make visitation with your grandchild difficult for you."

After a great deal of emotional discussion, the families agreed upon a plan. Devon's man-spread grew wider, and he steepled his fingers. He summarized, "Marty stays in school to finish his senior year. You take care of Elise's support. If there is a live birth, which should be next July after Marty has graduated, then we can have a paternity test done to see whether Marty is indeed the father. If he is, he can begin child support, with our help, if necessary. At that time, we can revisit the marriage question. I certainly won't entertain the idea of a marriage right now."

"For certain," Wyatt agreed. "We wouldn't want Elise to be saddled with a marriage to Marty if there's no live birth."

"Then we're done here." Devon rose to show the Evans family out.

They all rose to leave. On the way to the door, Rose inquired, "Do you want updates on the pregnancy?" The Parker men shook their heads no. Alice softly whispered, "I do."

...

If Marty was concerned about being the father of Elise's baby, he did not show it. He was dating Krista. He walked her down the school hallways with his arm draped around her shoulders. He drove her to and from school each day. They had lunch together in the school cafeteria where they huddled close, sometimes stealing a kiss, and often laughing with each other. Krista's ex-boyfriend, Todd, watched them from two tables over. He could not eat for the bile in his throat.

Elise experienced slight nausea each morning, but she was still in school. She planned to continue with her regular classes until the end of the semester in January. Although Elise's waist was thickening, Dr. Julie had informed her that she should be able to hide her pregnancy until the end of January, or early in February. By then she would be registered into a GED class to finish her high school education.

The winter break in December was a welcome relief for Elise. She was sick of seeing Marty hover around Krista. She was extremely tired and lacked the energy to do anything more than keep up with her school work. Wyatt offered to do the Christmas shopping for her. They chipped in together to buy Rose a mother's ring with their two birthstones plus a ruby for the baby's, and Joe a pair of pajamas and new slippers. Elise received baby clothes from her parents and Wyatt. They gave her baby blankets, frilly headbands, pretty, tiny dresses, and a delicate hand-crocheted sweater, bootie, and bonnet set. The receipts were kept in case the baby turned out to be a boy.

Elise was relieved to end the school semester mid-January and to begin GED classes held evenings at Maplewood Vocational School where no one knew her. She was less nauseated now, and she was beginning to feel a little more energy. Sleeping later in the mornings improved her attitude and her ability to concentrate on her studies. She found she could learn at a faster pace working on her own with the occasional help of the GED teaching staff, than she did in the regular classrooms.

An ultrasound at the end of February proved that Elise's baby was a girl. The Evans family enjoyed discussing possible names for her. Rose favored Rosemary in honor of her maternal grandmother. Joe was partial to Wynonna in honor of his mother. He also was fond of the idea of naming her after himself, either Josephine or Joellen. Wyatt was keen on Lindsay or Lynette. Elise agreed with the proffered names she liked, and nixed the ones she did not like, but she did not offer any names of her own. She smiled secretly, knowing that she had already decided on the name.

The doctor told Elise that her baby was already moving. In the first week of March, Elise noticed her kicking. By the end of March, she was kicking more frequently, especially when Elise attempted to sleep at night.

...

While Elise lost sleep due to her pregnancy, Marty lost sleep due to another pregnancy. Krista had told him she was two months pregnant. Marty was already in trouble with his father for Elise's pregnancy. Now he worried his father would find out about Krista. When Krista continually asked Marty, "What are you going to do about this?" he always answered, "I don't know."

At the beginning of her third trimester, Elise began doing the exercises suggested by her doctor to strengthen her pelvis area for an easier delivery. She expected to deliver mid-July.

While the Evans family waited for the birth of Elise's baby, Krista could no longer wait for Marty to offer a solution to her dilemma. At six months pregnant, she could not hide her baby bump. She told Marty she expected a wedding before the birth. When Marty would not commit, Krista showed up on the Parker doorstep wearing a tight skirt that showed off her baby belly. Mr. Parker was livid.

It was the end of July when Elise's baby made her appearance. Elise and Rose were home when Elise called to her mother from the bathroom. "Mom, I can't stop peeing! I don't know what's going on."

Her mother entered the room and immediately understood. "You're not peeing, Honey. Your water broke. I'll call the doctor. You grab your overnight bag." Rose also called Joe at work and Wyatt at school. She rushed Elise to the hospital. Both men arrived soon after they did.

Rose stayed in the labor and delivery room with her daughter. Wyatt quickly followed his father's hasty retreat when Elise began to shriek in pain with her contractions.

For twelve hours, Elise thought she might die in agony. If she had known child birth would be this painful, she might have opted for an abortion. Finally, the excruciating pains ended, and the nurse whisked her new baby girl away to be evaluated and cleaned up. Rose left the room to inform Joe and Wyatt that they were officially grandfather and uncle. The men rushed in to see the baby, wrapped tightly in her receiving blanket, being placed in Elise's arms. Elise, with sweaty gown and matted hair, smiled at her family. "You waited. You're the best."

She looked down at her red-faced little one and whispered, "Meet Jolene Rose."

...

Elise telephoned Marty Parker. "Our daughter has arrived. She's beautiful."

The Parker men refused to visit Elise in the hospital or to come to the Evans' home to meet Jolene Rose. Alice Parker did come to the hospital the day after Jolene's birth. She brought her a soft stuffed animal and cooed over the baby.

"I do think Jolene might have Marty's eyes, don't you?" she asked Elise. "She's beautiful."

Elise, as intimidated by Alice as she was by the rest of the Parker family, did not answer.

Alice continued, "I do hope that you and your family will allow me to stay in this child's life despite what Devon, uh, Mr. Parker, will decide to do. I know I should live by his ruling, but sometimes..."

Elise thought she knew what Alice meant. Elise sensed that Devon Parker was a controlling man who would not tolerate noncompliance with his authority. She thought Marty might model after his father and insist on complete control in a relationship.

She was not sure whether he was absolutely domineering or whether she had inadvertently given him total authority while they dated.

Alice stroked Elise's hair. "I always wanted a daughter. All my babies are boys. I want you to know I would take great pleasure from a relationship with you and Jolene. I do believe she is my granddaughter."

Elise felt her sincerity and reached out her hand to Alice. Alice took it and squeezed.

"Well, I want you to know that if you and Marty marry to give this little one a two-parent home, you will never have to worry financially. You're probably aware that Mr. Parker is a contractor and owns his own construction business. Marty will have a position in the company if he wants it, or we can afford his college for a different career path. Either way, the company will build you a beautiful new home. We did that for our other boys, and I'm sure we would do it for you and Marty. What a blessing to have your first home be more than just a starter home! Here, let me hold the baby for a while before I go."

Alice reached out and gently picked up Jolene from Elise's arms, carefully cradling the baby's head. "Come here, you little sweetie pie, and let your other grandmother hold you." She sat in the rocker next to Elise's bed with Jolene held tenderly to her chest.

...

It was not until after the paternity test proving Marty was the father that Devon conceded to meet the baby who was now three months old. He went alone to the Parker home. In their living room, he softened as he looked down at her. "She does seem to have Marty's eyes."

“Would you like to hold her?” Elise held Jolene out to Devon who shook his head no, but he did smile.

“I need to speak with your father. We have matters to discuss.” Devon left abruptly, beckoning to Joe on his way out. Joe caught up to Devon on the front porch. Elise wondered why matters concerning her and her baby were to be discussed in her absence. At this point, however, she felt she had no right to complain. She had caused this problem for both families, and she could only be grateful for the support she was receiving.

The two men faced each other, ready to negotiate. “Have a seat,” Joe offered, pointing to the whicker settee.

“You can see she’s my granddaughter,” Devon admitted. “I want her well taken care of.” He knew that finding a point where they agreed would be the best starting place.

“What do you have in mind?”

The basic plan was that their children would marry, live in the Parker home, the Parkers would support them, Marty would go to college, and Elise would finish her GED. The Parker Construction Company would build them a home when Marty graduated and began earning an income.

Joe was in agreement until Devon mentioned, “Of course, she will have to sign a prenup.”

Joe took the idea of a prenup as an insult and nearly ended the negotiation. He managed to choke out, “What would be in it?”

When Devon explained, Joe realized it would protect both parties. It would adequately provide financially for both Elise and Jolene Rose while protecting Parker family assets. “One more thing must be in there.” Joe pointed to Devon’s tablet where he was making notes.

Devon looked up. "What's that?"

"The house you're building for these kids. It has to be hers. To stay hers. I mean, if they separate or divorce, it has to be hers. I don't want that to be able to be taken from her, and the financial agreement stays the same. Otherwise, no prenup."

"You drive a hard bargain, but that can be done."

The two men shook hands on the deal.

...

After his discussion with Joe Evans, Devon Parker had an intensely forceful discussion with his son Marty. Marty was acutely aware that his father had the upper hand. His father owned the family business that brought them all prosperity. His father controlled whether he would pay for Marty's college, whether he would employ him in the business, and even whether he would eventually inherit. Marty's comfortable and somewhat luxurious life style was dependent upon his father.

Marty entered his father's study on command. Usually, he and his father sat in the two facing chairs in front of the oversize mahogany desk. Today, Devon pointed for Marty to sit in one chair while he remained behind his desk. Marty cringed at the stormy look on his father's face and sat. He knew enough to remain silent until his father spoke and gave him a clue.

"What the hell is wrong with you, son! I thought you were smarter than this!" Devon exploded. He placed both fists on his desk top and leaned toward Marty. "What were you thinking? Apparently, you weren't thinking with your brain!"

Marty squirmed in his seat and tried to guess what his father was talking about.

"How could you not have learned from your mistake? You've made two girls pregnant. Two that I know of. Are they any others?" Devon glared at Marty.

Uh, oh, he knows about Krista. How did he find out? "Sir?"

"Don't you question me! Give me an answer. You know darned well what I'm talking about. How many other pregnant girls can there be that you've been with?"

"Elise and Kristy are the only two that I know of, Sir." Marty forced himself to look steadily into his father's angry eyes.

"Two! Two that you know of. That means that you've been with others who could come forward. Well." Devon sat down, placed his elbows on his desk, laced his fingers in front of his mouth, and glared at his son. He let two uncomfortable minutes pass, building Marty's awkward self-consciousness.

"This cannot continue. This will not continue. I will not tolerate it. It will close too many doors in your future if your randyness leads to scandals. Then there's the expense of paying child support to a horde of mothers. This is what you're going to do." Devon folded his hands on top of his desk and steepled his fingers.

"As you know, that girl Elise had her baby. The paternity test is conclusive that it's yours. You're going to marry her and ..."

"But Dad, I don't love her, and what about..."

"Do not interrupt me. You are going to marry her, and that will help the other problem go away. The other girl can't demand that you marry her when you're already married. We can give her a one-time payment in lieu of child support with a non-disclosure drawn up by our attorney to keep it quiet. She should be delighted to accept that because, according to my private investigator, she's been seeing her old boyfriend, Todd Rogers. We'll offer a settlement that will make the two of them happy."

Devon continued, "If you're so randy that it causes these problems, you're better off married where it won't get you into trouble as long as you keep it at home. Now, this girl, this Elise, seems like an intelligent girl, maybe a trifle mousey, but pliable. She comes from a good middle-class family. She should make a suitable enough match for you."

Marty was frozen with aversion to the idea of marriage. He stared at his father, but he was afraid to interrupt.

"You can still go to college. You'll have to go locally, Hiram, Kent State, or Akron U. You can choose. You can live here in our finished basement until you graduate. Then you can find your own job, or you can work with me in the family business. The company will build you a house, a nice house, and give you a more than decent salary. You'll live in comfort and have a good life, but you'll live it married with a wife and a family."

"I don't think she loves me any more than I love her. She's the one who broke up with me. It isn't up to just you and me, Dad, she has to agree, and I don't think she will." Marty certainly hoped not.

"Son, I have faith in your powers of persuasion. You may need to court her again. I've had a talk with her father. He seems like a reasonable man. When he understood the financial security available for his daughter and grandchild, he agreed this is an advantageous plan. He even agreed to a prenup, so if she leaves you, she can't take what isn't hers. I did have to agree that we would build her a home, but the company was going to do that for you anyway, just as we did for your brothers. However, Evans demanded that we include in the prenup that it will be hers if you should divorce. I had to agree, or he would not allow her to sign a prenup. Our lawyers will draw it up. After they approve, I expect you to sign it, and I expect you to stay married and to be a decent husband. No scandals. Now, you won't see any more of this other girl, this Krista, or any other girl, is that clear?"

"Yes, Sir, but what about ..."

"My lawyer will be in touch with her. Don't contact her again."

"Yes, Sir. No, Sir." *Oh, shit.*

...

Elise felt pressured into a marriage she did not want. Her parents both wanted her to have the security offered by marrying into the Parker family. They also wanted a father for their granddaughter. Mrs. Parker encouraged her to become part of their family, and even Mr. Parker showed some softening toward her and Jolene. Her brother pointed out the financial hardship on their parents if they would have to bear most of the burden themselves, and the benefits for Jolene to be in the Parker family.

"You can always get a divorce if it doesn't work out," Wyatt told her. "I mean, I wouldn't normally feel that way because I think when you marry for love, you also have to have trust, but this isn't exactly normal. You need a father for Jolene, and security for you both. I'm guessing you could have a rather agreeable life, unless you really hate him?"

"No, I don't hate him. I just don't like him that much, but he has been treating me fairly well since he's been coming around again. I'm not sure how much he cares for Jolene. He doesn't pay her much attention."

Marty was persistent. He paid Elise more attention than he ever had. He brought gifts for Jolene. He took Elise to upscale restaurants and movies or concerts when her parents would babysit. Inevitably, Elise caved in to the pressure to marry him. She still carried some guilt at placing a burden on her family, and this would be a way to alleviate that burden. At least Marty seemed nicer this time, and maybe love would grow.

Love did not grow between Marty and Elise.

Marty married her in the chambers of a judge who was a friend of Devon's. He settled his new family into the lovely finished basement of his parents' four thousand square foot home. It was as beautiful as any main floor living space. There was a guest bedroom with a large closet that became their master bedroom. The attached bath had a stone-tiled shower and a double sink vanity with a granite top. Another guest bathroom was next to it. The Parkers supplied them with soft, luxurious towels, cleaning supplies, soaps, and shampoos. A smaller bedroom became Jolene's nursery. Hardwood floors flowed from room to room. French doors opening to a stone patio provided them with a private entrance. At one end, louvered doors closed off the utilities. At the other end, a full-sized refrigerator stood next to a wet bar with a microwave and a wine cooler. There was no stove, so they ate most of their meals upstairs with the Parker family. Elise was content to live there.

Marty spent most of his days at the university. He ate dinner with his family, then studied in his old bedroom upstairs. He explained that he needed the privacy away from distractions to study. Elise would take Jolene back to the basement.

Those nights that Marty would reach for his wife in bed at night, Elise wondered why people referred to it as making love. It did not seem loving to her, although it was the most intimate thing she had ever done. Marty had done more to create a longing in her when they were in high school. On the rare occasions that Marty took more time with her, she would respond to him. Other times it was a chore that she submitted to.

Alice invited Elise upstairs during the day when the men were gone. She and Elise enjoyed a blossoming friendship. Sometimes Alice would drive them to visit with Elise's parents, and sometimes her parents would come to visit at the Parker home. Elise felt that she had more in common with her older mother-in-law than with her high school friends.

Marty was seldom around. When he was home, he paid no attention to Jolene, and little to Elise. If the baby fussed, he either went upstairs to his old bedroom, or he left without telling Elise where he was going. He never changed a diaper or offered to help in any other way with the baby. That did not surprise Elise. Marty paid no attention to his several nephews during the noisy Parker family get-togethers.

Elise enjoyed those Parker family gatherings, although she never felt completely part of the family. She discussed child care and development with her sisters-in-law, and she chuckled at the antics of their children, but never was she invited to have additional social contact with them outside of those family times.

Elise's GED classes provided her with her only other social contacts. Those were limited to short breaks during the three-hour sessions twice a week. Elise realized that none of those friendships were strong enough to last after GED graduation. Their only common ground was their focus on their studies. She was correct in this. After passing her GED exam in January, she no longer had contact with any of them.

Alice wanted to plan a large graduation party for Elise. Marty told her not to bother. Joe and Rose took Wyatt, Elise and Jolene to a celebration dinner at the local Olive Garden. Marty stated he could not go, he had to study.

Jolene was Elise's biggest joy in life. Her baby was a precious gift. She loved to cuddle her and to play silly baby games with her. She spent hours teaching her Peek-a-Boo, Itsy Bitsy Spider, Buzzy Bee Came Out of the Barn, This Little Piggy. She pointed to her body parts and named them. One day, Elise began, "This is your nose…" and Jolene pointed to her nose before Elise did.

Excited, Elise tried, "This is your ear…" but Jolene just looked at her. She tried, "This is your mouth…" but Jolene did not point again for another month. When she did, she did most of them correctly and giggled. Elise dashed upstairs to share the achievement with Alice. Alice was suitably impressed and drove them to the Evans' home to show off for Elise's family. When Marty was told, his bland response was, "That's nice," and he went to study.

Before Jolene could talk, Elise counted to her. She counted fingers, toes, shoes, socks, cereal bites, crayons, books, items from her purse, trees in the yard, toys in the tub, people in the room. She read her stories, taught her animal sounds, took her for walks and pointed out objects. She looked online for developmental activities for babies and toddlers and used them with Jolene who became a precocious toddler.

Each milestone was celebrated by Elise, her family, and Alice Parker. Marty's typical response was a bland, "That's nice." When she took her first steps he warned, "Keep her from getting into things," before he walked away. Devon Parker was not home much more than Marty, but he was sometimes interactive with Jolene. He was developing a soft spot for his little granddaughter. He was not unkind to Elise, but she continued to feel like an unwanted guest in his home. She asked for nothing from the Parkers. They were supplying her with a home, meals, and her husband's college.

While Elise's marriage was less than she had hoped for in her life, she felt fulfilled as a mother. She could not be happier with her daughter. She lived in a beautiful home with the promise of another beautiful home of her own in the near future. She felt love from her own Evans family, and she had a pleasant friend in Alice Parker. Without having her own money, and without having to ask for anything, she had everything she needed. She knew life could be better, but she also appreciated all she had. It could be much worse.

When Marty graduated with a business degree in computer science, he began working for the family contracting and construction business at a more than decent starting salary. Devon was true to his word and asked Marty what kind of a house he wanted.

Without conferring with his wife, Marty answered, "About three thousand to thirty-five hundred square feet, hardwood floors, four bedrooms, four bathrooms, a study, a man cave, traditional."

Elise, who had never asked the Parkers for anything, surprised them now by saying, "That would be too much house for us. Around two thousand square feet, or maybe a little more, would do, and only three bedrooms and three bathrooms. I want two large walk-in closets, a modern tile fireplace in the living room, a three-season sun room, large windows with the blinds built inside. I want a wrap-around porch on at least two sides and a patio out back with an open- air complete kitchen built in under a roof. The indoor kitchen should have granite countertops and an island, all open concept with hardwood floors. I want a two or three car garage off to the side, not in the front, and I want a car. Marty needs to buy me a car, a new one, so it's reliable."

The Parkers looked at her in astonishment. They had thought she was a pliable mouse of a girl, but she was now showing some spunk. Elise felt the house was Mr. Parker's responsibility to pay off on his promise to her before she married his son. She had no qualms in asking for what she wanted when it was owed to her. Now that Marty was earning their keep, she had no problem in asking for a car, which was going to be more necessary when they moved into their own home.

"I watch HGTV and I've been looking at plans in the Sunday paper and online. I kept a few that I really liked. Mr. Parker, I'll show them to you, and you can advise me on the ones that are the most suitable. I'll respect your judgment."

This was how Elise's first house came to be her dream home.

...

They found an eight-acre site to build their new home. Marty double-checked all the subcontractors' work. Devon did his own monthly inspections. Elise approved all the finish products. They moved in the summer when Jolene was five years old.

That fall, Jolene started half-day kindergarten. It broke Elise's heart to wave good-bye to her daughter mournfully waving back through the school bus window. It did help when Jolene began to look forward to going to school.

One crisp October morning, Elise looked out the bedroom window when she first woke up. She had to rub the sleep from her eyes to understand what she was seeing in her front yard. There were three horses grazing on her well-manicured lawn. She quickly threw on her robe and woke Jolene.

"Come on, Honey, Mommy wants to show you something outside." Wrapping a blanket around her still sleepy five-year-old daughter, she carried her outside. Indeed, three horses were just outside their front door contentedly munching grass. One brown head shot up to eye the humans standing on the porch while it continued to chew. The other two horses turned their butts to the humans and otherwise ignored them.

"Look, Jolene. Do you know what they are?"

"Uh huh, they're big." Jolene stretched out her little arm pointing at them.

"Those are horses. What sound do they make?"

"Neigh, neigh," Jolene answered, sounding not at all like a horse.

"Yes, that's right, a horse neighs. How many horses are there?" Elise pointed as Jolene counted to three.

"You are so right! What a good, smart girl you are. Let's go in now and get ready for school."

"No, Mommy. See the horses." Jolene was fascinated with the large creatures. Elise would have carried her to them to pet them, but she was not sure if they were safe.

"I'm sorry, Honey. We don't want you to miss your bus. We'll hurry so you can be ready before it comes and we can watch the horses then." Elise turned back to the house, and Jolene turned her head for a last look at the horses as she was carried inside.

That day, Jolene wanted to stay home from school until Elise told her she could tell the other children about the horses in her front yard. Elise put her on the school bus and waved good-bye.

Their neighbor on one side had horses that Elise had never paid attention to. She walked over to the fence running the length of the shared property line and noticed the gate on the other side was open. No cars were in their driveway, so Elise felt like she was on her own to return the horses to their pasture. As she attempted to walk up to one of the horses, it moved off. She tried a second horse, but it, too, moved off. She tried the third horse, which stood looking at her. Tentatively she reached out to pet it. The horse snorted and Elise jumped. When she jumped, it jumped and moved away from her.

Man, they're big. What am I supposed to do?

She approached the last horse again and urged it to follow her. "Come on big guy, let's go back to your house." She took a step toward the horse pasture, but the horse did not follow. Elise was afraid to go behind the horse and push. Hesitantly, she gently pushed the horse's left shoulder and it took a step to the right. *Umm, I wonder if that was a coincidence.* She gently pushed on the horse's right shoulder and it took a step to the left. *Umm, I may be on to something.*

By pushing the horse's shoulders, she kept his head aimed toward his home pasture, but she could not find his buttons to move him forward. The other two horses would not allow her to come close to them. *I know! Carrots! They like carrots, don't they?*

She grabbed two carrots from the refrigerator and found a piece of rope in the garage. "OK girl, or boy, or whoever you are, you're supposed to like carrots. Try this one." With one hand, she held out the carrot, and from the front side of the horse she looped the rope around its neck with her other hand. The horse turned its head toward her to snatch a bite of carrot. *My arms aren't long enough. I can't stand back here to hold the rope and still reach the carrot far enough in front.* Elise dropped the rope and moved to the front of the horse, holding out the carrot. The horse took a step forward and seized another bite. "That's the way. Good girl! Keep going."

As they made their way toward the neighbor's pasture, the other two horses began to follow them. Elise was afraid they would crowd her for the carrots, but they plodded along in single file. Once through the gate, Elise closed and latched it. The carrots were gone. *It's amazing what you can do to train a horse when you have carrots,* she thought.

After that, Jolene kept asking to see the horses. They would walk over and feed them pieces of apple or carrot across the fence. Elise found children's library books about horses and ponies to read to Jolene. Both of them became more fascinated with equines. The next summer Elise found a couple of horse shows in the area and took Jolene. Just before school started, they went to the county fair. On the Midway, there was a vendor taking pictures of children on a sad looking saddled pony. Elise asked Jolene if she wanted to sit on the pony. Jolene was eager. "Yes, Mommy! Up!" She raised her tiny arms in the air.

"Just a minute, Honey. Mommy has to buy some tickets." After the photos were taken, Jolene did not want to leave the pony. She wanted to ride it.

"No, Jolene, you don't ride this pony. It stands here for pictures, but there are other ponies over this way that you can ride. Should we go see them?"

Jolene was thrilled to ride a short Shetland pony around the circle. She was having so much fun that Elise paid for three turns.

When Marty arrived home from work, Jolene scampered to him to tell him about her day on the ponies. He brushed her aside and asked Elise when dinner would be ready. "Fifteen minutes. Sit down and relax. It's almost done."

"We'll tell Daddy about the ponies while he eats his dinner," she proposed to her disappointed daughter.

During the meal, Jolene was all smiles as she talked incessantly about the ponies. Marty ignored her after saying once, "That's nice."

How this man is missing out on enjoying his daughter! I guess he was never made to be a father. How sad for him. Elise looked at her husband she did not understand, did not love, but depended on. *How sad for all of us, but especially for you and Jolene.*

Elise did not dislike Marty, she just did not like him. He was not unkind, just indifferent to both her and Jolene. Jolene's Uncle Wyatt and her Grandpa Evans were better father figures in her life, and they made sure to be there for her often. Jolene remained a happy child, close to her mother. They attended most of the Parker family gatherings, but Marty did not go with them to see the Evans family. He did not care what they did, where they went, or how long they were gone. It was not that he supported their activities, it was that he was uninterested. They had their lives and he had his.

...

Jolene was eight when Wyatt began taking his sister and niece camping to a place in Cook Forest State Park in Pennsylvania. Uncle Wyatt wanted his niece to experience the pleasures of the natural outdoors. They cooked all their meals over an open fire and made s'mores for dessert. They hiked a couple of trails each trip, and either canoed or kayaked down the Clarion River. The highlight for both Elise and Jolene were the guided horse-back rides from the livery stable at Ray Smith's Cook Forest Scenic Trail Rides. Ray kept decent, reliable saddle horses and they enjoyed the beauty of the forest lands while also enjoying the horses.

When Jolene was ten, she asked her uncle if they could go camping more often than once a year. "I always hate to come back home. The forest is so beautiful, and I love the horses."

Elise felt the same way, but she knew that her brother only had two weeks a year vacation time. She did not want them to impose on him. However, she had an idea brewing in the back of her mind. At Ray Smith's they had watched people camping with their own personal horses and horse trailers. Why not them? Then they could go on their own as often as they wanted. She needed to do some research.

Marty was no help. When she told him about her idea, he responded, "Do it if you want to, but leave me out of it."

Wyatt and Joe researched horse trailers and towing vehicles. Joe found a local farm that gave riding lessons. Elise signed up both Jolene and herself for weekly lessons. At that barn, she ran into some young girls who belonged to the Portage County Ohio Horseman Council, and she joined the club to have more access to horse activities and events. The OHC was organized by county chapters to build and maintain horse trails in Ohio. Most members owned their own horses, but it was not a requirement. Elise began attending the OHC meetings and events with Jolene. She began to learn more and more about horses, horse care, trailering, and horse camping.

At a Parker family gathering, Elise asked Devon to have the company build her a small horse barn in her back yard. After seeing all the remodeling and building that the family business did for the other family members, Elise did not feel out of place to ask this smaller favor. Devon agreed. Elise showed him the barn plans, and it was built within the month. Jolene was beside herself with excitement.

"This means I'm getting a pony, right Mom?"

"It's one more step on the way, Sweetheart. We still have some research to do. We have to find the right kind of horses for us. The people in the club will help us out. They know we're looking."

By summer, Elise felt knowledgeable enough to buy two older, well-broke horses with many miles of trail experience. Wyatt helped her to find a suitable used horse trailer and an appropriate truck. He sat in the truck cab with Elise, instructing her on pulling the empty trailer before she put her horses in it. He made sure she was proficient at turns and backing before giving his approval. Someone in the OHC club sold her a used saddle, and she bought a new saddle from Carl's Tack Shop. Carl helped her select everything else she would need to care for the two horses.

At first Jolene and Elise rode only with the OHC group. It did not take long until Elise felt experienced enough to go on day rides on her own with Jolene. Jolene was an intelligent girl who had learned a lot about horses along with her mother, so she was a big help. Marty said not a word about the initial expenses of the horses, or about paying for their ongoing care. Elise suspected that he welcomed the prospect of the two of them being gone more often. She also wondered if he had a guilty conscience for not being a loving husband or doting father and was trying to make it up to her.

Jolene was the happiness in Elise's life. Even so, not having a loving relationship with her husband left a hole in her heart. She felt a loneliness, an emptiness, that no one else could fill. It was not that she loved Marty and wanted a closeness with him, per se, but she felt the void of not being able to love, to trust, to share with a devoted partner. She craved passion, tenderness, respect, and caring with someone who loved and cherished her.

...

Elise was twenty-nine years old and Jolene was fourteen when they met Nancy.

2 LAVERN

The happiest years of Lavern Esser's life were her school years, especially high school. She was popular and involved in school activities, and she still had her family.

Lavern did not have a best friend. She had many good friends, and the respect of most of the other students.

She was popular because she included everyone in her smiles and conversations. The jocks had their click, as did the cheerleaders, and the newspaper and yearbook staffs, the band, and the pretty girls with the pretty clothes. Lavern fit in with everyone because she spoke to everyone and refused to shun anyone for not being in one of the "in" groups. Other kids were afraid to speak with those deemed lesser than themselves for fear of losing their own status. Lavern had empathy for those who were not popular and tried to include them when she could. She did not feel she belonged to any one segregated group, but rather to the school as a whole. She was a Ravenna High Raven.

In study hall her junior year, a sophomore boy, Freddie McClean, cradled his head in his arms on the table across from Lavern, who was doing math homework. She thought he was sleeping until he suddenly looked up at her and whispered, "How far up do you shave your legs?"

Kids sitting on either side of him snickered. No one else seemed to hear. Lavern knew Freddie was considered socially unacceptable. When Freddie turned red and quickly put his head back down, she knew he was embarrassed that he had committed another social gaffe. She gently touched his arm across the table and whispered, "Freddie, men don't ask girls or women personal questions, no matter how curious they are about them. Someday you'll be married, and you'll find out some answers. Don't worry about it now." She gave him a gentle tap on his arm before removing her hand, hoping it signaled that she was not offended.

In gym class, when she was made captain of her volleyball team, she alternated calling for the athletic girls and the unpopular girls to be on her team. When she called the name of Lyn Taylor, who was more than chubby, the girls she had already picked groaned. Lavern gently told them to hush. "It's only a game. Don't make anyone feel bad."

She had a mild way about her that chastised others without offending them. It brought them up short and reminded them of decencies and graciousness. She brought out the best in others who otherwise might have tended to be rude and offensive.

When Lavern heard kids gossiping that if Alice Chambers was elected to class treasurer, she might steal the money, Lavern asked them not to repeat those hurtful thoughts because they would start a rumor that could hurt Alice for years to come. "You don't have any proof, do you, that she's a thief?"

"Well, no, but look at her. Look at how she dresses. You know she doesn't have any money. What an opportunity to get some, to be treasurer," Billie May spoke for the group, and the others nodded in agreement.

Lavern did not give up. "Do you think dressing the way she does deserves a label of being dishonest or a thief? How would she feel if she heard you talking this way, or a rumor of this sort came back to her? Come on now, none of you want to be responsible for that."

Two in the group rolled their eyes at each other. The other three hung their heads and agreed Lavern was right.

Lavern made a point of seeking out Alice to wish her good luck in the election. "You would make an excellent class treasurer," she told her. "You're really gifted in math."

When the captain of the dance team told McKinsey Alltop she could not try out for dance club because she was deaf, Lavern suggested they allow her to dance at the try out. "If she has dance skills, we want her. She should be able to keep the beat from the bass notes, you know, the bass vibrations. Let's not say no because she's deaf, only if she can't dance."

It turned out McKinsey was a more than adequate dancer. She had taken dance classes since she was three years old and had moves the other girls did not know. They brought her into the club and managed to communicate with gestures when McKinsey was unable to read their lips. McKinsey knew American Sign Language and used an interpreter during the school days, but the interpreter left at three o'clock. The other dancers began to learn some of the more frequently used signs.

One of Lavern's favorite high school activities was the drama club. They acted out silly skits for school assemblies. The good-natured laughter of the students gave her a thrill. She told her family that she must be a ham.

"I wish I could see you in some of those skits," her younger brother, Ray, told her.

"Well, everybody, guess what?" she asked her family. "I made it for a part in our class play. I want all of you to come to one of the performances!"

"Oh, we will, we will," Ray shouted.

Her mother, Wendy agreed. "Of course, of course. Congratulations. Mark it on the calendar and we'll all be there."

Her father, Vern, gave her a hug. "That's my girl, a bright and shining star. Yes, we will be there, Princess."

Lavern loved her family. They always supported and encouraged her. She did the same for her brother Ray, gently guiding him through some of his difficulties and praising his successes.

Preparing for the class play was intensive. There were lines to learn, rehearsals to attend, and scenery to build. As an actor, she was not expected to build sets, but she volunteered anyway. One Saturday, the stage crew was to meet at ten in the morning, but only Lavern and Sally Scott showed up. The auditorium of the school was separated from the rest of the school building by a long hallway. The doors to the hallway were closed, locked, and chained. They had entrance to the auditorium and its stage, but not to the rest of the school.

"I wonder if anyone else will be here?" Lavern asked between sips of the large cola she had ordered from the drive-through window of McDonald's on her way.

"They better be. We don't want to do all this by ourselves today," Sally grumbled, flipping her hair. "Let's finish our drinks and get to work and hope they come soon."

Lavern and Sally worked only an hour when they needed to use the restroom. "Sally, I'll be back. I need to go. That cola was too big."

"Wait, I'll go with you. I had a large drink, too, plus orange juice and coffee at breakfast. I'm ready to burst."

The girls jumped off the stage and approached the doors leading down the hall to the main part of the school building. That is when they noticed the chains.

"The doors to the school are chained!" Sally moaned. "The restrooms are in the other part of the school!"

"Oh, my gosh! What are we going to do? I'm ready to burst, too."

"Yeah, and we're here where there aren't any businesses around to use their restrooms. We're really stuck … unless, did you drive?"

"No, my father dropped me off on his way to take my brother somewhere. He's supposed to pick me up at three o'clock. We can't wait that long."

The girls began laughing. "What are we laughing for?" Lavern asked Sally. "This is becoming dire! It's starting to hurt."

"Yeah, that's for sure. Hey, we could pee into our empty drink cups." Sally picked her cup out of the trash can and studied it, wondering if it would hold all her urine. It would be difficult to stop in mid-stream if the cup filled up.

"I think we're going to have to. It'll be better than peeing our pants which is about to happen, but what if the other kids start coming and see us peeing into our cups? Oh, my gosh, we'd never live it down. It's too embarrassing, but I've got to go!"

"OK," Sally agreed. "This is beyond uncomfortable and into painful. Let's crouch down in a row of seats, and maybe if someone comes they won't notice us."

"Oh, please don't let anyone come," Lavern prayed as she pulled down her jeans in between the seats and crouched over her soft drink cup. "Ahhh! Relief." Her stream stopped just as her cup was about to overflow. "Are you done?"

"Yeah, I'm done. Thank goodness no one came. Hey, what are we going to do with these cups now? We can't put them into the trash. We can't leave them around here."

"No problem. Let's go outside and throw out the pee, and then we can throw the cups in the trash."

Lavern experienced no other problems while working on the play, until the last evening of the performance. Lavern's character was on stage. The lead character played by Billy May was sitting on the sofa. Lavern was standing near an end table with a telephone on it. Billy's brother, Tommy, the sound man, was a practical joker. He had been playing pranks on the cast and crew all during rehearsals. Now, in front of the audience, he made the phone ring. Lavern and Billy looked at each other, eyes wide. This was not in the script. Lavern, who was closer to the phone, answered it.

"Hello?" Slight pause, "No, you have the wrong number," and she hung up. Billy continued with his scripted dialog. They could see Tommy silently laughing backstage as the play continued. The second time Tommy made the phone ring, she answered, "Hello? Oh, yes, he's here. It's for you," and she handed the phone to Billy who searched frantically for something to say.

"No, no, I don't want any, and I'm asking you not to call again," Billy yelled into the phone, hoping that his brother would understand that the words were meant seriously for him. "I'll deal with you later," Billy added into the phone before hanging up.

At curtain call, her father handed her a bouquet of red roses. Her family waited to talk to her and congratulate her before she left with friends for the closing night cast party. They were proud of her, and she basked in their love and support.

...

Lavern had always been an animal lover. Her family visited the zoo several times over the years. She was not allowed to own a dog, but she did rescue several strays and find the original owners when she could, or a permanent, loving home when she could not. She fed the stray cats in the neighborhood. Once she found a baby bird in the front yard after a windstorm. The bird was naked, pink, ugly, and pitiful. She placed it in a box and fed it worms she dug up. When it developed into a robin with feathers, she had it perch on a stick and moved the stick up and down in the air until the tiny thing flapped its wings. Slowly, she taught it to fly. One day in the yard as she worked with it, it took off into the trees. It never returned. Lavern hoped she did the right thing by it.

Once, when her family went to the circus, she decided that horses must be the most beautiful creatures on earth. She would have asked for one, but she knew her family could not keep one where they lived in the city.

During her senior year in high school, her friend, Marci Davis, asked her if she would go with her to an event in Columbus, Ohio, called Equine Affaire. "It's a huge horse symposium. You like animals, and you said you like horses. Well, there are so many horses there. I mean, like, it's all about horses," Marci told her. "They have national trainers there all day working with horses in arenas, like, all over the fairgrounds. Yeah, it's at the Ohio State Fairgrounds. We can choose whatever we want to see. Like, every hour there're eight or ten different sessions. Come on and go with me. It'll be fun. My mom promised that if you go, we can have our own hotel room right next to hers and Dad's."

"What kind of things will they be doing with the horses?" Lavern wanted to know before she would commit to asking her parents for permission.

"Oh, anything you can think of having to do with horses. Like teaching a misbehaving horse to have ground manners, barrel racing techniques, starting a young colt under saddle, trailer loading, stuff about eventing, reining, dressage tests, drill teams, vaulting, just all kinds of stuff. You can go through the horse barns, and you can see the breed showcases. It's really fun. Plus, there're lots of vendors, like more than a thousand. Bling, bling, bling! Bring some money."

Lavern did not know what all of that was, but it sounded interesting. It would be a chance to have some fun hanging out with Marci and to see horses up close. She asked her parents, who questioned her extensively about Marci's parents. Finally, her mother called Marci's mother and after talking with her, Lavern received permission to go on the weekend trip.

Equine Affaire was held Thursday through Sunday, but both girls were in school, so Marci's parents drove them to Columbus after her father was off work Friday evening. They arrived in Columbus at eight o'clock and checked into the hotel where they had adjoining rooms reserved. Marci wanted to keep the adjoining door closed, but her mother said, no, it would stay open. Marci pouted, but Lavern told her it was fine, they were only going to be watching tv before going to sleep.

The next morning, they ate the breakfast provided by the hotel and drove to the fairground. It was only fifteen dollars admission to see everything with one exception. There was an extra ticket needed for the evening performances called Fantasia. Lavern had no idea what that entailed. The family had tickets, including one for Lavern. Marci's sister, who was away in college, had backed out of going because of a huge study load, which gave Lavern her opportunity.

They were each handed a program on the way into the fairground. "Come on, let's look at the schedule." Marci was enthusiastic. As the four of them studied the schedule for the clinics and demonstrations, a plan developed. Marci and Lavern would take off to see the ones they were interested in and meet her parents in the indoor food court at twelve-thirty for lunch.

They walked along the outside food vendors smelling cinnamon, popcorn, sausage, grilled onions and peppers, and other delightful food odors. Marci took her to the building called the Coliseum for their first clinic. It was presented by a trainer Marci informed her was nationally known. It was called Foundation First, about starting the young horse from preparatory ground work to completing a successful first ride. Lavern was entranced by the whole training sequence of positive reinforcement. She whispered to Marci, "I thought the cowboys saddled up while the horse was held down, then rode them until they submitted and quit bucking."

Marci chuckled. "No, no, most everyone uses modern techniques today. This makes a partner of your horse instead of breaking his spirit. Isn't it cool?"

"Yeah, it's really interesting to see how the horse figures out what it's supposed to do and ends up doing it willingly."

Toward the end of the clinic, the trainer had saddled and bridled the horse as it stood still without being tied. Because there was not enough time left, he announced he would ride it for the first time in his clinic the next day. "I don't train by the clock, so sorry if I disappointed you folks. I let the horse tell me the time it takes to go to the next step, and it seems this one was a little slow." The crowd laughed. Most of them were wowed anyway by how much was accomplished in the hour and a half clinic. Lavern was fascinated by the communication between the trainer and the horse. The trainer had explained to the crowd each signal the horse gave, and the reason for each of his own moves. *I would love to do that,* Lavern thought.

Marci's parents attended seminars on equine eye diseases, pasture management, equine first aid, hoof care, and barn safety. The girls went to training seminars on exercises to improve control over your horse's body, developing a novice western pleasure horse into a finished show horse, how horses learn and think differently than people do, and how the natural instincts of the horse relate to training.

Lavern was fascinated. It seemed that each seminar tied in to what the others had to say, working with a horse's instincts instead of against them, and using positive reinforcement. One trainer explained, "It's making the right thing easy and the wrong thing difficult for the horse until it decides to do the right thing. Pressure and release. That's the key. Put pressure on the horse until he does the right thing, and quickly release the pressure as its reward."

They only had time to see a fourth of the vendors. They met Marci's parents for supper in the indoor food court, then stood in line for the special Fantasia show. They had reserved seats, but the doors of the Coliseum were locked after the last clinic, and would not open until seven o'clock. As the crowd was finally allowed to enter, music was playing, adding to the expectant mood. When most of the people were seated, someone in a section across the arena from the Davis group began a wave. The human wave traveled around and around the huge Coliseum as the crowd laughed and hollered and waited for the show to begin.

The program began with several horse-pulled buggies, carriages, and wagons delivering the American flag and a soloist to lead the crowd in the national anthem. Next was a Roman rider, a lady riding two horses at once by standing with one foot on the back of each horse. She drove four other horses in front of the two she rode in a six-horse hitch. They galloped around the arena to loud and frenzied music. Lavern nearly stopped breathing when a crew member placed a jump in their way. The two lead horses sprang up and over, the second pair cleared, then the rider on her two horses. The crowd cheered and Lavern breathed again.

A gorgeous Trakehner, all black and very tall, was ridden by a man in top hat and tails for a dressage performance to music. The horse kept the beat to the music as it marched in place, did a lead change with each step, side-passed, crossed the arena on the diagonal, and did other maneuvers that Lavern did not recognize. Its floating trot was full of impulsion and suspension. It seemed that the rider sat perfectly still, but Marci assured Lavern that he was signaling the horse through his seat and his thighs. The dressage made Lavern want to cry with its beauty.

The drill team made her want to holler and shout. The music was fast, and so were the horses. There must have been fifty riders galloping into the arena, horse manes and tails, and rider hair streaming behind as they raced into various formations. They circled, paired off in twos and sometimes threes or fours, blended circles into two lines that galloped toward each other and passed through each other every other horse. Lavern would have held her breath, but she was too busy shouting.

She found out what the vaulting was when a troupe led in a large dapple-gray Percheron to trot steadily around a ring while the young people in the troupe took turns jumping on its back and striking a pose before dismounting. Sometimes two or more would create a pose on the back of the horse as it continued its steady trot. The riders were sideways, backwards, standing, kneeling, climbing on another's shoulders. It was all so graceful.

One of Lavern's favorite performances was an act with twelve white horses at liberty. The trainer stood in the arena with two whips, one short, one long. She would signal her horses with the whips and they would move around her singly, or in pairs. She had them bow and rear to command. It amazed Lavern how they would do her bidding with no lead line.

The free-style reining was a crowd pleaser. The western rider did a routine to music that included flying lead changes, sliding roll-back stops from a full-out gallop, and spins in both directions. It was all fast action to fast music and lots of fun.

Also fun was the trick horse routine. Marci told Lavern the trainer had taught a clinic on trick training your horse on Friday before they arrived. "I wish we could take off school to come all four days, because we miss some good stuff," she told her.

The final act was the little Icelandic horses doing their specialty, a fast, smooth gait called the tolt. The riders had worked out a drill pattern, but the real crowd pleaser was when they all exited the arena only to return one at a time and race break-neck speed in the gait called a flying pace, carrying their riders smoothly across the entire arena from entrance door to exit. The crowd roared for each rider.

The show was over, but Lavern was smiling. "Did you have a good time?" Marci asked her as they made their way down the steps.

"Oh, my, yes. Thank you so much for bringing me here. It was awesome!"

"Now, tomorrow we can scout the rest of the vendors, see some more clinics, and watch the versatile horse and rider competition."

"What's that?" Lavern put her hand on Marci's shoulder so they would not be separated in the crowd.

"It's a whole obstacle course set up in the Coliseum. It's a contest for speed and accuracy for anyone who wants to enter with their horse. They have to do all kinds of things with their horses. It's a hoot to watch. We don't have to stay for the whole thing, though, 'cause it's long and there's so much else to see. I'm glad you're having a good time."

Back at the hotel and worn out, they fell asleep immediately.

The next day, after a clinic in the Voinovich Livestock and Trade Center building, they were walking through the breed pavilion where horses representing about twenty breeds were stabled. Marci thought it would give Lavern a chance to learn about various horse breeds. What caught Lavern's eyes were two babies stabled in the Last Chance Corral booth.

One was a brown and white spotted fellow on wobbly legs. The other was tan with a darker brown mane, tail, and stockings. They were so cute with their fluffy hair and short manes sticking straight up. One of the Last Chance volunteers whose name tag said, "Judy," allowed Lavern inside the stall to cuddle with one of the babies. She hugged the gangly brown filly who tumbled into the sawdust and ended up in Lavern's lap on the floor. Lavern fell in love. She was horrified to learn both babies were orphans and to hear the plight of the babies called nurse mare foals.

Volunteer Judy explained how the Last Chance Corral was created to rescue abused, neglected, and otherwise unwanted equines. As Judy leaned against the stall door, she looked at Lavern on the floor and told her, "The rescue of the nurse mare foals has become our main program. The nurse mare foals were only born so their mothers, the nurse mares, could come into milk for an industry that supplies surrogate nurse mares for other foals that can't nurse from their own biological mother. Once the nurse mare foals are born, their job in life is over. They are a throw-away by-product."

Lavern hugged the little foal closer. "How sad."

Judy continued, "The nurse mare is then leased out to raise a different, more valuable foal. Although anyone with any breed of horse can lease a nurse mare, eighty-five percent are leased for Thoroughbred foals in the racing industry."

"Why are so many nurse mares needed?" Lavern asked, looking up at the volunteer.

"Well, nine days after giving birth, a mare comes into estrus. No Thoroughbred can race in this country unless they were conceived by live cover, so, the Thoroughbred mare will then have to travel to the stallion to be rebred. Her valuable foal cannot accompany her safely, and by the time she returns, her milk will have dried up. Therefore, a nurse mare is hired to raise the Thoroughbred foal. The nurse mare's foal is a by-product and is therefore considered disposable. Most are killed."

Judy turned to talk with other people.

What fun it would be to take this little one home to love and to train the way we saw in the clinics yesterday. Lavern decided to find out how to adopt the filly so she would be armed with all the information before going home to plead her case to her parents.

Lavern looked up at her friend. "Marci, if I would adopt one of these babies, where could I keep it?"

"Are you serious? You don't really want one of these, do you? Do you realize how much work they take? I mean, like, it would be a huge commitment. Aren't you just thinking impulsively?" Marci stood on one foot, then the other. "You've never owned a horse before. Don't try to start with a baby. Wait 'til you know what you're doing. Come on, let's go finish looking at all the vendors." She turned to leave, but Lavern was not ready.

"Wait, give me a minute." Lavern stood and brushed sawdust off the seat of her pants. "I want to talk to these people first."

Marci sighed as she stood aside to allow Lavern to exit the stall.

There was a small crowd around the booth in front of the stall. A different volunteer was answering questions. "The Last Chance Corral contracts with several of the race horse farms to purchase as many of the foals as possible for a nominal fee. Once purchased, the foal is rushed to the Last Chance Corral to be stabilized before being adopted to a loving, forever home."

A man wearing a western hat, western shirt, and large, shiny belt buckle asked, "What are the adoption requirements?"

Lavern listened with dismay as she learned she would have to already own a horse and have an established relationship with a veterinarian and a blacksmith who would need to vouch for her. She also struck out by not having a barn and pasture on her own property. She still felt drawn to the small, fragile lives an industry was so quick to slaughter, so she donated the twenty dollars to Last Chance Corral that she had intended to use to buy a necklace or bracelet for herself.

Marci tugged on her arm, and Lavern finally walked away with her.

Lavern hastily snatched a brochure that included the website lastchancecorral.org for future reference. Maybe she could spend some of her summer vacation volunteering to help with the barn and feeding chores.

As they wandered down the aisles of vendors in the Bricker building, Marci told Lavern about the farm where she boarded her horse. "You know, if you really want a horse, you could board it where I keep mine at Buckeye Farm. Slade, the owner, is a superb horseman. He takes care of his property, and he watches out for all the horses boarded there. If he sees someone not treating their horse right, he talks to them about it. He has strict rules for safety, but that's for the good of the horses, and the people, too, I guess. He's like, actually kind. He like, helps any of us with any problems our horses might have."

Marci picked up a bracelet to admire, and Lavern thought about the twenty dollars she just gave away. *Oh well, if I had another twenty, I would give them that, too,* she knew.

"His place would be perfect for boarding your first horse. You'd end up learning a lot from Slade. If you decide to get into horses, come out there with me. You'll see." Marci put the bracelet back and they strolled to the next booth to check out the framed art work.

...

Lavern was surprised when her parents did not give her a flat out "no" when she brought up having a horse. She eased into the subject by telling them many times about Equine Affaire, Last Chance Corral, and how she enjoyed the horses. It was mid-May when she delved farther into the subject of horses and broached owning one of her own.

"We figured you would come around to that," her father, Vern, admitted.

"We've been wondering what special thing we could do for your high school graduation, and we thought perhaps finding you a horse of your own would be perfect," her mother added, as she stirred the family's evening dinner on the stove top.

"Hey, yeah, I vote for that!" Ray was enthusiastic. "Can I ride it, too?"

"Wow! I didn't think it would be so easy." Lavern had to sit down. She was overwhelmed. "Can we go see Slade, where Marci boards her horse, and talk to him? She assured me he could help us find a good horse and teach me how to care for it. Marci would help me, too."

"How about Saturday morning after breakfast?" her dad asked, already knowing the answer.

"Oh my gosh! Yes! I'll call Marci for directions. Maybe she could meet us there, too." Lavern took off for her bedroom to call Marci with the thrilling news. She stopped just outside the kitchen, turned, and yelled back, "Thank you, thank you!"

"Just a minute, young lady," her mother only half scolded. "There will be some ground rules. You start college in the fall and the horse cannot interfere with your studies. You have to keep up your grade point average to keep the horse."

“That’s right,” her father agreed. “The horse is to be a stress reliever. You have to keep up your grades. That’s first and foremost. Then, too, we want you to contribute financially to the horse board. So, with a part-time job, your class load and studies, along with time for the horse, you won’t be able to join a sorority.”

“That’s agreeable, Dad. I’ll do my best in school. I really want to be a teacher, so I need to have my college degree. That will affect the rest of my life, so I promise I’ll finish school with the highest grade point average I can.” Lavern dashed off to make her call to Marci.

“Wow,” Ray grinned, “that’s a cool graduation gift! Can I have a car when I graduate?”

…

Slade Meyers, long and lean, a widower in his late seventies with children out-of-state, enjoyed the young people who boarded their horses at his barn. He was indeed helpful. Knowing Lavern’s interest in training, he found a mare just coming two years old. Lacy was a rich brown Chestnut with black mane and tail, halter broke to lead, but she did not lead respectfully. Slade told her ground manners would be the first order of training. “You’re constantly training,” he told her. “If you’re around the horse, you’re teachin’ her somethin’, even inadvertently and unknowingly.”

“You have a lot of training to do before you even think of ridin’ her, but I’ll tell you what. That mare is a good-goin’ horse. Just watch her move out in the pasture.”

Lavern smiled.

Slade continued, “In fact, you should take your lawn chair to the pasture and hang out with her. Watch her for as many hours as you can. See how she interacts with the other horses. See what all you can learn about natural horse communication." He spit tobacco juice.

Lavern figured she would enjoy doing that all summer before starting full-time at Kent State University.

She had signed up for one summer class at the university, Early Childhood Development. Her summer routine became driving her father to his work on her way to campus for her morning class, grabbing a quick lunch at home, driving to the barn to see Lacy, and leaving there in time to be back in Kent for her job. She had found an evening job working five to nine at a coffee shop Mondays through Fridays. If her mother needed the car, she would drive Lavern to the coffee shop, and one of her parents picked her up after work. Her father's friend from work dropped him off at home. She studied for her class at night and often was not in bed until midnight or later.

Slade was usually busy around the farm when she arrived, so Lavern would set up her lawn chair in the pasture to observe Lacy and the rest of the horses as they grazed or stood head to tail swishing flies off each other. She began to recognize the signals they gave each other to communicate. When Slade was free, Lavern would approach Lacy and lead her to the round pen for ground work training under Slade's supervision.

For the first session in the round pen, Slade had Lavern remove Lacy's halter and lead rope. She trotted off, stood still, and turned to peer at Lavern. "Remember that the horse is processing everything you do for meaning. Be aware of your body and control your movements. You want to show her you're the boss mare, not her, and earn her respect."

Slade handed Lavern a whip. "Have her move off by cracking this behind her. You don't need to touch her. She'll move." He went on to explain how Lavern should position her body to the horse. Lavern cracked the whip and Lacy, startled, jumped forward into a gallop. Slade had Lavern keep the horse moving for several revolutions of the round pen.

"Now allow her to stop. Stand still. If you stand still, the horse can stand still. Arms to your side, head down, relax and don't move. See what she does."

Lacy slowly brought her speed down to a trot, then to a walk. She turned her head to the rail and gazed over the top.

"She wants to be out of this situation and away from you. You want to create a relationship where she wants to be with you more than anything, where she gives you her attention and focus. Move her off again. If she looks at you as she's runnin' around, stop and be still. It'll be her reward for giving you her attention. You're makin' the wrong thing hard and the right thing easy."

Finally, the horse gave Lavern her eye, and Slade yelled, "Stop!" just as Lavern dropped her head and arms and stopped her feet. "Good timing, Missy," Slade praised. Stay still now until she looks away. Then make her go back to work when her focus leaves you."

Lacy dropped her head and licked her lips. Slade said she was thinking over this turn of events. "Give her a rub on her neck or shoulder."

The session continued until Lavern learned to turn the direction of the horse around with her own body position, and Lacy was watching Lavern with both eyes. The next day they reviewed. Lacy was quicker to respond to Lavern's non-verbal requests to stop, to change directions, to stand still and keep her eyes on Lavern. Next, Slade showed Lavern how to make Lacy do inside turns toward her instead of the outside turns toward the rail as Lacy had been doing.

"All right, Missy, you're both doin' good," Slade told her. Lacy stood looking at Lavern and licking her lips. "Her inside turns are more respectful of you, and this whole thing is showing her that you can stop her, make her move, and make her turn either inside or outside. You should have her respect by now and be deemed worth following. Let's see if she thinks you're her leader." Slade spit. "Now turn your back and slowly walk away from her."

Lavern walked to the other side of the round pen and was surprised that Lacy walked right behind her.

"That's it, Missy. She's joining up with you, giving you the respect of being her leader. Walk around. If she stays with you, just keep walking. If she moves off, make her go to work again running around. You'll be cementing in her mind that near you is the best, most comfortable place to be."

Lavern walked around the round pen with Lacy following her without a lead rope. Lavern snapped the lead to Lacy's halter to take her back to the barn. She was now leading respectfully. Lavern kept Lacy in position behind her right shoulder. If something would make Lacy spook forward, she would not run over Lavern. When Lacy occasionally tried to walk past her, Lavern would twirl the end of the lead rope so that Lacy would bump her nose into the twirling rope and quickly back into place. Slade told her, "It's not you hitting the horse, it's the horse runnin' into the twirlin'rope. She already knows where she needs to be in relation to you. Your job is to be consistent and insistent to keep her there."

"Make the wrong thing difficult and the right thing easy, huh Slade?"

"You bet, Missy. You're a quick learner."

...

Each day Slade would give Lavern an exercise to work with her horse. He would watch her closely and correct every detail such as her body posture, where she pointed her feet, where her shoulders pointed, to puff out her chest or collapse into a relaxed position. It was more difficult than Lavern had imagined it would be as she concentrated both on Lacy and on herself. She was grateful for Slade's help.

Slade met her at the round pen and opened the gate for Lavern to lead Lacy inside. He latched the gate behind them. As she stood in the middle of the sixty-foot circle, he told her he would show her how to put "buttons" onto her horse.

"You're going to create spots, or buttons, on your horse that will each have a different meaning so you can communicate with her. When you ask your horse to do a certain thing each time you touch a certain spot, and it starts to do that each time you touch her there, then you have a "button" to touch to have the horse do that movement. On the ground, you'll use your crop, or your hand, to tap the button, and in the saddle, you'll use your feet. You see then, this ground work will transfer to the saddle."

Lavern nodded her understanding. *Sort of.*

"You want control of your whole horse. Your first button will be about four or five inches in front of where the girth goes to control her shoulders. The second button will be immediately in front of the girth to control her rib cage. The third button will be behind the girth to control her hips."

"OK, unsnap your lead rope."

Lavern hung the lead on the rail of the round pen gate. Lacy trotted away, stopped, and snorted at the sand.

Slade continued the lesson. "Don't look at her eyes or head. Look at her hips, puff up your chest, and walk toward her with energy as you stare at the button behind the girth area."

Lacy responded by trotting off.

"Bring your energy down, but keep your chest puffed up and walk slowly toward her, staring at that third button. You can point the crop there, and if she still doesn't move her hips, lightly tap the end of the crop on the spot."

This time Lacy moved her hips away from Lavern's approach as she held her ground with her front legs. "Does this mean that it worked to use her button?"

Slade refused to answer. "You tell me. What do you think?"

"I think I'll try it a few more times, then tell you." After a few more times moving her mare's hips with this method, Lavern answered, "I think I'm communicating with my horse."

"Yup, you're becoming the boss mare. Be consistent. She'll want to know every day if you are the boss or if she is. If she moves your feet, she's the boss. If you move her, you're the boss. Remember, that includes any time you're around her. So, if you're groomin' her and she moves into you, keep your feet still while you move her back."

One day, Slade told her they would work on a turn on the haunch. "Keep the lead rope on her. Stand slightly behind Lacy's barrel. The goal is to have her cross her front legs while rotating her body around her back legs. Touch the first button, the one a few inches in front of where the girth will be, the spot that controls her shoulders."

The mare stood still.

"OK, touch with more pressure until she moves. As soon as she crosses her front legs and begins to turn around her rear, release the pressure, drop your head, relax and reward her with a pet."

Three more times Slade had Lavern practice turning Lacy with just one crossed step in front before immediately releasing the pressure. Next, he told her to ask for two steps before the release. When he felt Lacy was understanding the ask, he told Lavern to release after three steps. In small increments each time, the horse ended up doing a three-hundred-sixty degree turn on the haunches before the release. Then Slade had her teach the same thing to Lacy in the other direction. "Like teachin' a whole new horse. Tomorrow we'll review this and start on the turn on the forehand."

The turn on the forehand was the opposite of the turn on the haunches with the horse rotating its body around its front legs by crossing its back legs. This time Slade had Lavern stand at Lacy's shoulder and put pressure on the third button behind the girth area that controlled the hips. As soon as Lavern applied enough pressure with the crop that Lacy took her first crossed step in the turn on the forehand, Lavern released the pressure, relaxed her posture, and rubbed her horse's neck.

"That's the way, Missy! You've got your timing down. Do that a couple more times, then ask for two steps before releasing the pressure."

It wasn't long before Lacy did an entire rotation in a turn on the forehand.

"That's enough for today," Slade advised. "Put her away for a reward. Don't keep practicing 'til she's bored or starts messing up. You can work on both these turns for about ten minutes each, every day, until she's doing them with a minimal tap of the crop. You're doin' a good job with this mare. And don't feel it's a waste of time to start with all this ground work. It will transfer over to the saddle when the time comes."

"Oh, no, Slade, I'm loving this. It's interesting. It's fun. I do want to ride her, but this is wonderful stuff I would never have known without you. I mean, I watched trainers at Equine Affaire do some stuff similar to this, but I wouldn't have been able to do it on my own without your help. Thank you so much for all the time you've given me."

"My pleasure, Missy, my pleasure," Slade told her as she led Lacy toward the pasture.

Another day, Slade told Lavern to walk Lacy in a circle keeping the mare in position just behind her right shoulder.

"OK, OK, that's good. Now we're goin' to make her soft to bend. Slide your hand down the lead rope toward her face 'til she bends her nose in toward you."

Lavern stopped walking and slid her hand toward Lacy's face.

"No, keep walking in your circle. Release her nose when she bends in toward you. The release of pressure is her reward. That's it! Now do it again and release as soon as she bends her nose toward you. Yeah! Good timing. Now do that a few more times but ask her to hold that bend for a few seconds before you release."

After a few minutes of this, Slade instructed, "Now she's giving you her nose willingly, so next we're going to ask for her neck. Same thing. Slide your hand down the lead until she gives you her nose and her neck. Keep walking your circle."

As soon as Lacy put the bend in her neck, and Lavern released her, Slade told her, "She has it. She's figured it out. See her lick her lips? Give her a moment to think, then work her from the other direction. Ya always have to train both sides of a horse's brain, just like they're two different animals."

Lavern watched Lacy lick, then drop her head to snort at the sand used for the round pen footing. She then turned Lacy to walk a circle in the other direction. When she was bending her nose and her neck toward Lavern when asked, Slade told her, "She did it right. Now go put her up in her stall to think about it. You always want to quit when they've achieved something correctly. It's a reward, and I do believe they think about what happened. Never overwork your horse to the point it gets bored or starts makin' mistakes after doin' it right. Tomorrow we'll do a quick review and ask for nose, neck, ribs, and rear. Yup, she's goin' to be a nice little mare for ya."

Over the next two days, Lavern walked her horse in a circle, slid her hand down the lead rope asking Lacy to bend toward her. When she had a bend in nose, neck, rib, and rear, Slade hollered, "Stop now. Stop your feet. Let's see if she'll side pass from there. Bump button two just in front of her girth area. If she moves her ribs away, she should side pass."

When Lacy did not move, Slade advised, "Add a bit more pressure until she does move. She'll get it."

When Lacy did not side pass, Slade was not rattled. "When teaching your horse something new, and it doesn't do what you ask, don't blame the horse. It's more likely you're not communicating in a way it can understand, rather than the horse is being stubborn. We're going to try a different technique."

Slade moved the pair from the round pen to the end of the side of the barn. "Stand facing the barn. From there with you on her left, she can't move except backward, or sideways to the right like we want her to. We'll side pass along the line of the barn, then you move to her other side so she can side pass to her left on the way back."

"What? All at once?"

"No, no, Missy. In increments, same as before. One step and reward then build. So, you're on her left, you want her to move sideways to the right. Bump that third button behind the girth. If she doesn't move, increase the pressure. There! Release! Did you see her crossing her feet? Work up to three steps in each direction and put her up. I have some stuff to finish, but you can work on your own. You have the timing, the pressure release, down real good. Work on the turns on the forehand and the haunches and on the side pass this week, everything from both directions. I'll have a look at her next week to see your results." With that, Slade walked away.

Lavern was proud that Slade thought she was ready to work her horse without him standing over her. While she was somewhat uneasy, she also felt ready.

When Lacy would side pass the length of the barn from the first ask with just a slight touch, she took away the crutch of the barn and worked her on the gravel drive, in the paddock, in the pasture, in the round pen. She reviewed all Lacy's lessons with her in many different places. Slade had told her to train in a variety of places so that Lacy would be sure to connect the cue to the request rather than to the place it was first taught. "We want her to respond correctly to the cue wherever she is, not just in a round pen."

Lavern had her family come to Buckeye Farm to watch the progress of the training. Her parents were impressed. Ray wanted to know when he could ride.

"We're starting to prepare her for that tomorrow," Lavern answered.

They began by slowly introducing the saddle blanket, then the saddle, then the bridle to the horse, step by step. When Lacy was tacked up, Lavern sent her around the pen to become used to wearing the saddle and bridle. At first, she bucked and farted. When she settled down, dropped her head, and licked her lips, Lavern put her weight in the left stirrup for only a second. The horse stood still, so Lavern tried it for two seconds. Slowly, she built the time standing in one stirrup to thirty seconds. When Lacy continued to accept her weight there, Lavern laid across the saddle like a sack of potatoes. When Lacy moved off, Lavern could slip to the ground unhurt. When Lacy stood quietly each time Lavern placed her weight across the saddle, Slade had Lavern mount the rest of the way, briefly rub Lacy's neck, and dismount. When Lavern mounted, Lacy looked back at her as if to say, "What are you doing up there?" She never bucked.

Slade gave her instructions on how to ride. "When you ride, look forward to a point ahead. Keep her in a straight line. Sit up straight. Don't lean the way you do on a motorcycle. Feel her body. Know what part of her body is where. Have her stop by setteling your seat deeper in the saddle and bringing your energy down." When he felt it was safe, he allowed her to ride Lacy outside of the round pen. "Work on your backups. Put a reliable back up on that horse. Every time you stop, have her back up two or three steps. That will result in a good stop. Work on the side pass from the saddle using your feet to bump her where you did from the ground for her cues."

It was a great summer, the last happy summer Lavern would have for a long time.

...

The summer class ended, and Lavern had two weeks before her full-time class schedule began for the fall semester. Instead of seeing her horse more, she decided to work with Lacy in the mornings and spend the afternoons with her mother and brother before having to go to work for the evening. She felt as though she had been ignoring her family over the summer. She missed them. After her work at the coffee shop, she would come home and sit on the front porch to talk with her father. She was pleased that she lived close enough to Kent State to live at home while going to school. She would miss her family if she had to live in a dorm on campus.

She signed up for Educational Psychology, Early Adolescence, and her general courses in the fall. In the winter she took Educational Technology, Professional Practice, Curriculum and Organization, and the rest of her general courses. She planned on graduating in three and a half years by taking a summer course each year, but she never had a chance. It became more important to work a summer job. Continuing her education at all became questionable.

It happened the end of February. It was one of those super storms that dumped two feet of snow that partially melted, turning the top layer to ice overnight.

Ray and Vern had shoveled out the Esser driveway, and highway crews had cleared and salted most of the main roads. Vern did not want Lavern to drive, so he dropped her off at the university and drove himself to work. He told her he would pick her up in front of the student center building at six o'clock with the rest of the family, so they could go to Ray's junior high school basketball game together. Lavern had covered for a co-worker last weekend, and that girl was working Lavern's shift tonight. Lavern would study until two in the morning if she had to, not to miss the family outing.

They never came to pick her up. She kept watch on the parking lot from the glass doors of the student center, but never saw the family car. She thought her father would send Ray up the concourse to the building to get her if she did not see them, but Ray never came. Finally, at six-thirty, she braved the frigid wind and hurried down the concourse to the large parking lot to search, but they were not there. Worried and clutching her books, she hurried back to the warmth of the building where she called their cell phones. No answer. She called home. No answer.

Lavern gave them another fifteen minutes and called the police. "I don't know if this is an emergency. I'm sorry, but I'm worried about my family. They were supposed to pick me up over an hour ago, but they never showed. I don't know what to do." Her voice was constricted with fear and came out in a near squeak.

"What is your name, Ma'am?" the dispatcher asked.

"Lavern Esser." She set her load of books down on the floor.

"How many family members are missing?"

"My mother, father and brother."

"Their names, please?"

Lavern told the dispatcher.

"Where does your family live?"

Lavern gave the address and added that no one answered the phone there.

"And where are you located now?"

"In the student center building at Kent State."

"Yes, Ma'am, please stay on the line. I'll get right back to you."

Lavern shifted from one foot to the other, wondering what the dispatcher was doing. She came back on the line in less than three minutes.

"Do I understand that you need a ride home?"

"Well, I don't know. I guess. I mean, my family was supposed to pick me up, but they didn't come. I don't know where they are."

"Yes, Ma'am. A squad car is on its way to pick you up and take you home. What part of the building are you in?"

Lavern told her. “But I need to find my family. Maybe they went to my brother’s junior high basketball game and just forgot to pick me up. No one is answering their phone. I’m worried about them. I don’t know what to do.” A sob turned into a hiccup.

“Yes, Ma’am. The officers will be there in just minutes. They will help you. You can stay on the line with me until they arrive.”

Two uniformed officers, one male and one female, entered the building just then. Lavern told the dispatcher they had arrived, thanked her, and hung up. She waved at them before picking up her books. The woman spotted Lavern first and pointed her out to her partner. They approached and asked her name.

“Lavern Esser. I’m the one they sent you for. Do you know where my family is?”

The officers introduced themselves. “We’re here to help. Come with us.”

Lavern was too stunned to speak as they hurried across the concourse in the freezing, blowing wind. The policewoman helped her into the warm squad car, and they began to drive.

“Where are we going? Are we going to Ray’s school to see if my family went to the basketball game without me? Do you know where they are?”

The policeman was driving. He pulled over at the outer end of the parking lot and half turned in his seat. “Look, Miss Esser, uh, Lavern, this isn’t easy.” He glanced at his partner who took over for him.

“We are truly sorry, Lavern, but we know your family was in a serious car wreck, probably on their way to pick you up.”

"No!" Lavern wailed. "Are they all right? Is everyone all right? Is anyone hurt?" She clutched at the grill between the front and back seats, her heart beating too fast and a foul taste in her mouth. "Tell me everyone's OK. Where are they? Can you take me to them?"

The man cleared his throat. The woman gave the rest of the painful news. "I'm sorry, but the family in the silver Toyota Highlander did not survive."

In shock, Lavern did not hear the rest of what the policewoman was telling her.

"The ID in the man's wallet was for Vernon Esser. The ID in the woman's purse was for Wendy Esser. There was a young teenage boy in the car with them. We need you to come with us to identify the bodies, unless there is someone else you could send to identify them? Is there anyone we could call to do that for you, or to meet you at your house? Or is there somewhere else we could take you?"

The officer had to repeat the questions several times to break through Lavern's stunned fog. Even then, she could barely sob out her answers between great gasps for air. "No, I, I, um, I have to go. I have to see. It's not them! No, no! Noooo! Noooo! It can't be! Noooo!" She sobbed, she screamed. Tears spilled down her cheeks. Her nose ran.

It can't be them. This is a nightmare. No, I'm here, but it isn't real. Something else happened. It was someone else's silver Highlander, someone else's family. Noooo! Not her family, not her sweet little brother Ray, not her wise and loving father, not her devoted and caring mother.

"Nooo! It can't be! It just can't be!" Lavern beat on the grill, oblivious to the bruising it caused on her hands. The policewoman came around from the front to sit in the back seat with her. She hugged Lavern close and told her partner to drive to the hospital. The bodies were in the hospital morgue, and the doctors there would give Lavern a sedative, and perhaps keep her overnight.

After identifying her family, Lavern was heavily sedated. She was released the next day with a prescription for a sedative. Marci and her mother came to pick her up. They filled the prescription on the way to their house.

"You're staying with us for a while, young lady," Marci's mother, Marsha, insisted in a tone that allowed no argument. "You have no other family. We can help you make funeral plans and arrange your insurance payout on the car. Once that comes, you can buy a car of your own and maybe go back to your own home." She looked in the rear-view mirror at the red-eyed zombie sitting stonily next to Marci. "Meanwhile, we could never allow you to manage all this on your own." She hoped that Lavern's parents had a will.

"Thank you, Mrs. Davis," Lavern whispered with no inflection.

"Call me Marsha. We're all willing to help. This is such a tragedy. Do you know if they had life insurance or a prepaid funeral?"

Silent tears trickled down Lavern's face. Marci did not know what to say. She patted her friend's arm.

Marsha asked Lavern whether she preferred one funeral home over others. Instead of answering, she broke down in tears. Marsha decided to handle most of the funeral on her own. She called a home and made an appointment for early that evening. The funeral director asked if they would hold three separate funerals. "No, I think one for the three of them. I doubt this poor girl would make it through three."

Before they left for the appointment, Lavern informed Marsha, "I have to go home. There's a metal box in my parents' bedroom closet. They told me to open it if anything ever happened to them. We need to get it."

They picked up the box on the way to the funeral home. It had her parents' will. If one was to die before the other, the surviving spouse was to receive everything. If they would die within a month of each other, the two children would inherit everything equally.

The car title and car insurance policy were both there, and the deed to the house along with mortgage documents. The box also held a small life insurance policy on Wendy. Marsha thought it would pay for her burial. There was a larger insurance policy on Vern, but non for Ray or Lavern. Marsha thought the funeral and burials for the three would be covered by the two policies with not much left over.

"This is helpful, Honey. We know the amount we have to work with."

Lavern nodded silently.

She could not remember the appointment at the funeral home, and she could barely remember the calling hours or the funeral service, as muddled as she was with shock, grief, and medication.

Marsha gave Lavern two days to rest before setting appointments for her with the lawyer who had drawn up her parents' will, the car insurance agent, and the dean of the College of Education at Kent State. "You have to take care of this business, Honey. I know it'll be difficult. If you want, either Marci or I could go with you, or you can borrow our car. You do need to get the ball rolling on your business."

Lavern felt embarrassed for imposing on the Davis family, but she borrowed their car. The lawyer told her that the will would have to go through probate to be settled. The car insurance payout would go to the estate and be part of the probate. He would handle the paperwork for her.

The auto insurance agent told her he had inspected the wrecked Toyota Highlander and declared it a total loss. Lavern shuddered to think of her family inside the wreck and was relieved she did not have to see the vehicle. The company would mail a check directly to the lawyer for the estate.

The dean was fully understanding. She would receive incomplete status on each of her classes unless she was able to catch up before the end of the semester. He encouraged her to return to her classes soon and meet with each of her professors on how to make up the missing work.

She stopped by the coffee shop on her way back to the Davis home and told them she would be back for her shifts starting Monday evening. She would use the bus system to go to school and to work. She hoped the estate would be settled soon. She had only eighty dollars in cash with a small paycheck due Friday. She needed the money from her parents' checking and savings accounts to pay for utility bills, house mortgage, horse board, and spring classes. She needed a car to job hunt. The money in the bank accounts would not last long. Marci took her to Buckeye Farm each time she went to see her own horse, but Lavern missed seeing Lacy every day. She needed a car.

By the time the estate was settled, Lavern had made some decisions. She contacted a realtor and listed her family home for sale. She could not afford mortgage, maintenance, insurance, and utilities. Instead of a car, she decided to buy a used truck that would eventually pull a horse trailer to take Lacy on trail rides in the many northeast Ohio parks. *Probably not until I finish school and have a teaching job.*

Slade waited on her board money until the will was probated. She paid him up-to-date. He helped her find a decent used truck capable of pulling a loaded trailer. She found two other part-time jobs that allowed her to keep her job in the coffee shop on week-day evenings. On Saturday and Sunday afternoons and evenings she worked as a waitress at the Red Lobster where the tips were excellent. Her classes were on Mondays, Wednesdays, and Fridays, so she could work at the campus book store on Tuesdays and Thursdays until time to go to the coffee shop. Before taking on the other two jobs, she had been able to catch up with her courses and manage a 3.5 grade average. She studied late into the night and on weekend mornings. She lost weight and had dark circles under her eyes. She seldom saw her horse.

When the house sold, she put most of the money into the bank to be used for her education and to be sure she could always pay her horse board. The insurance money was gone after paying for the funeral and burials. She had to earn that degree! She wanted it for herself and because her family had wanted it for her. Instead of renting an apartment, she hunted for a used horse trailer she could park at Slade's and live in all summer. She found a somewhat rusty but serviceable stock trailer. She held a tag sale to sell most of the items in the house, keeping a few possessions that she moved into a storage unit. She took bedding and clothing to the trailer and began living at the farm. It saved money, and she was up early enough each morning to see Lacy before school or her book store job. She had no time to train or ride.

...

Instead of going to summer school, when the semester ended, she extended her hours at the Red Lobster, the best paying of her three jobs. She wanted to be able to rent an apartment when the weather turned cold. *Well, not an apartment. A room. I'll rent a room near campus.* For now, she lived out of her horse trailer. She showered in the women's locker room on campus and ate at the coffee shop and the restaurant where she worked. It was saving her money for now, but there would be no way to heat the trailer in the winter.

The fall semester started and Lavern had to cut her hours at the Red Lobster again. She read her assignments sitting in a lawn chair in her trailer reading far into the night by lantern light. She typed her written assignments on her laptop. When her battery died, she moved her lawn chair inside the barn and plugged into the electric outlet there. By mid-December she had spent some cold nights in a sleeping bag on an air mattress on the floor of her trailer before she gave up and found a room to rent near campus. Studying became much easier at the small dinette next to the bed. She missed seeing Lacy each morning and night.

In mid-April, she let the room go and moved back into the horse trailer. *I won't be even half-way through school until this spring semester ends next month, and never did I expect it to be so hard! I'm just so tired!*

Lavern contemplated not signing up for fall classes, but she had to make it through school to become a teacher. She did not want to be a quitter, give up her dream, and dishonor her parents' memory. She studied her budget to figure how far the rest of the money from the sale of the house would take her. She had applied for a partial scholarship, but she refused to apply for a student loan. She would rather live in austerity than to accrue interest. She determined that if she were awarded the scholarship, she would quit the coffee shop and book store jobs and only work the more lucrative weekends at Red Lobster. The idea made her feel better. If the scholarship did come through, she would even have some time for Lacy. She would have prayed for that, but she thought God would never listen because she was so angry with him for allowing her family to die.

Classes ended with Lavern managing a four-point grade average which helped her win the partial scholarship that would begin in the fall. She thought perhaps God was watching out for her after all, and she gave a quick prayer of thanks. She turned in her notice to the coffee shop and the book store. This would be an easier summer working only one job.

During her last week at the coffee shop, Charlie Smith came sauntering in on Monday evening. He was a new customer, muscular, handsome, somewhat older than the college boys, cocky. He had come roaring up to the curb on his motorcycle and allowed the door to slam closed behind him. Lavern was working the bar alone. He immediately began flirting with her in his soft, New Orleans drawl.

She ignored the flirting. “Let me know when you’re ready to order.” She turned and finished refilling one of the coffee machines.

Charlie was surprised. Most women were flattered by his attention. He ordered an espresso and watched Lavern as she made it. Liking what he observed, he sat at a table where he could watch her as he drank his coffee. He tried to initiate a conversation with her, but she would not engage.

When some of the regular customers came in and expressed their disappointment to hear she was leaving and to wish her good luck, Charlie realized he wanted to see her again. He came back on Tuesday, ordered an espresso, and tried to talk with her. She answered his questions with brevity.

He returned on Wednesday, ordered his espresso, and told her about himself. She listened. He tried not to brag, but he wanted her to know he made good money in computer sales, had an apartment east of Kent, enjoyed riding his motorcycle, did not drink much alcohol, liked music concerts, and did not have a girlfriend at the moment.

“And why is that?” Lavern finally asked him a question.

"Uh, the last one, uh, we weren't connecting well enough to get serious, and we mutually decided to end the relationship that wasn't going anywhere." Charlie looked down, picked up his cup, and took another sip. At closing, he asked her if he could walk her to her car.

"I have a truck, and no, I'll be fine, thank you."

What Charlie did not know was that Lavern thought about him Wednesday night and all day Thursday. When he came in Thursday night they had their first real back and forth conversation. She allowed him to walk her to her truck after closing.

On Friday, they both knew it was her last day at the coffee shop. She thought she would never see him again. He wondered if she would agree to date him. That night Lavern opened up a little about herself, telling him she was half-way through to her degree in education, that she had a horse she adored, that she worked at the Red Lobster. *There. Now he knows how to find me, if he wants to.*

He walked her to her truck at closing. "What time do you start work on Saturdays?"

"Right now, I'm working from eleven 'til seven every day."

He leaned on her truck and twirled his keys. "How about I pick you up tomorrow morning and we go for a spin on my bike?"

He looked so hopeful that Lavern almost agreed. Instead, she told him she did not have time to date.

"Well, now, ya see, sometimes ya just have to take some down time to make life worthwhile. Come on sweetheart, I really want to see you again." He glanced up at her through his long lashes and her heart melted.

She was embarrassed to tell him she was homeless and living out of her horse trailer to save money for school. She did agree to see him again for a night ride on his bike after work Saturday night. "You pick me up at the Red Lobster for a quick ride, then bring me back there to my truck."

The next evening was warm and musky with the smell of early summer flowers and damp earth. Lavern enjoyed the ride on the back of the bike with her arms around Charlie. When he returned her to her truck, he blocked her door and leaned in for a kiss. She returned it passionately, but then pushed him away with both hands on his chest.

"I'm sorry, Charlie, but I can't get involved. I have school and my job, and I don't even get much time with my horse."

"Sweetheart, you need to slow down." He took her arms and turned her back against her truck, and placed his hands on her truck on either side of her. She was caught with him inches from her. He kissed her long and slow. "Goodnight," was all he said as he released her and sauntered to his bike. He put on his helmet and watched as she climbed into her truck and drove off. He thought about following her to see where she lived, but then he thought better of it.

Lavern wondered if that were the end of it. It was not. It was only the beginning. On warm nights, he would pick her up at the restaurant, and they would ride the bike to West Branch State Park, dismount, and sit on a picnic bench in front of the lake. He told her about growing up in New Orleans, how his mother died of an overdose, and his father was an alcoholic. "He's the reason I rarely drink. I don't see him anymore. I guess I have no family until I start one of my own. I do want to do that, you know."

He looked so downcast, Lavern took his hand. She told him about how she lost her family. He held her while she cried. She finally told him how she was living in her horse trailer where she boarded her horse. "Don't feel sorry for me, though. I have some money set aside from the sale of the house. I choose to live cheap so I can use the money for school. I have two more years left."

That night she told him the next time he could pick her up at Buckeye Farm. He asked to go out there the next morning and take her to breakfast before her shift at the restaurant. "I'll take you to work on the bike, and pick you up after."

Lavern agreed.

When she introduced him to Lacy, she could tell he was not interested in horses. When he saw where she lived in her horse trailer, he was impressed with her courage and perseverance. By mid-summer he was asking her to marry him. "We could be our own family."

She told him no. "Charlie, I won't have much time to see you when the fall semester starts. I'm taking a full load again."

"Darlin', you can marry me and quit school. I'll take care of you. Quit your job, too, if you want."

"No, Charlie. I've wanted to be a teacher since I can remember. I'm going to finish. It's been long and hard, so I have to finish to make my sacrifices worth it."

"Marry me and you can stop sacrificing. I'll take care of you."

Charlie would not give up. In August, when there was a cooling of the night air, he told her she could not stay in the trailer over the winter.

"I know, Charlie. I never did that. I rented a room in Kent by campus."

"Darlin', marry me and you'll share my nice warm apartment and my nice warm bed."

Lavern admitted to herself that it did sound tempting. She enjoyed Charlie and thought she was in love with him. Her life would be so much easier joined with his. She told Charlie that if she married him, she would want to keep working at the Red Lobster on weekends and stay in school full-time. "Also, you would have to understand that I love my horse, and I would never give her up."

"Wow, are you saying yes?"

"Yes, I guess so, if you agree to my horse and my education."

Charlie agreed and bought her a ring. They were married in front of a judge with the Davis family as witnesses.

The honeymoon period was blissful. When Lavern was ready to register for her fall semester, Charlie lost some of his charm. He began to badger her to quit school. "We could use the tuition money for other things. You're married to me now. You won't have to teach."

Sometimes he complained about the times she would drive to the farm to see her horse. "Why don't you spend that time with me?" he whined.

She would gently remind him of his agreement.

"Come on, quit school, sell the horse, and let's make a baby. We need to grow our family. You can quit your job, too."

"I do want to have children, Charlie, but not until I've been teaching for a couple of years. Please don't badger me about the horse and school. You agreed."

Life with Charlie was sometimes difficult, but life with Charlie was easier than it had been on her own.

...

Lavern was twenty-three and beginning her teaching career when she met Nancy.

3 BRISTOL

As far back as she could remember, Bristol James had two recurring dreams, neither of them pleasant.

Throughout her childhood, Bristol had slept in hand-me-down nightgowns. They were always shabby, with frayed hems, threadbare fabric, and a tattered hole or two.

Her first dreams were of walking into the coat room of her grade school class, removing her winter coat, and finding herself still in one of her ragged nighties. She was so mortified, it would wake her up. Sometimes she would climb out of bed and find something to wear the next morning and lay back down dressed for school. That was not always easy because her mother allowed the laundry to pile up for two or three weeks at a time, and young Bristol had no clothes in her drawers or closet. On those mornings, her mother would hunt for the cleanest dirty clothes to wear to school while Bristol ate her breakfast. Either way, Bristol entered her grade school classrooms wearing unkempt, wrinkled clothes.

These dreams ended when Bristol insisted on wearing shorts and T-shirts to bed. When her mother, Elizabeth James, packed the summer clothes away in the fall, Bristol dug her shorts and T-shirts back out and continued wearing them to bed. She also began doing the laundry each weekend and ironing her clothes for the week. While no longer disheveled, she had no new clothes of her own, and nothing that was in the current fashion trend. She wore hand-me-downs from her older sister, Lucy. Her mother refused to buy her new clothes, telling her they could be hand-sewn for far less money. Elizabeth took Bristol and Lucy shopping for patterns and fabric, but after selecting enough for one outfit each, the purchase was put away "Until I have time to get to them." The outfits were either never made, or only Lucy's choice was made, or they were both made for Lucy.

When Bristol complained, Elizabeth justified sewing Bristol's choice for Lucy. "Your sister's only three years older than you, so you can have all of her clothes when she's finished with them. She's just a tad larger than you, so they'll be just fine for you later, and you'll be wearing your choice then, so hush now. You're lucky I get any time to sew at all. If you were smarter, you'd learn to sew yourself."

Bristol wondered how she was supposed to learn to sew when her mother never bothered to teach her, and she never understood why her mother was too busy to care for the family. Elizabeth did not work outside the home. She spent her time on social activities. She talked on the phone for hours, or visited with the neighbors, having coffee and gossiping. She joined the Parent Teacher Association and became an officer. She was in a bridge club that played monthly, a lodge that met twice a month, a church circle that met monthly, and a weekly bowling league. She taught a children's Sunday school class and spent several hours preparing her lesson each week. What she did not have was time to take care of her family. Elizabeth rarely cleaned the house. Bristol, Lucy, and their father Lester James, were always happy when it was

Elizabeth's turn to host the card club because she went into a cleaning frenzy, and the family enjoyed their spruced-up home.

Bristol was miserable each Sunday sitting in the classroom while her mother taught the Sunday school lessons. Bristol was always used as a negative example to explain the lessons. The other children would turn and stare at her. She would turn red and hang her head with embarrassment. She felt exposed the way she did in her dreams of arriving at school in her torn nightgown. After complaining numerous times on the drive home from church, her father had Elizabeth arrange to teach a different Sunday school class.

Lester explained, "Bristol, because it bothers you so much when your mother teaches your class, she will now teach the junior high class. Mrs. Jenko will be the new Sunday school teacher for your class. You won't have to be bothered anymore."

Bristol was still mortified thinking of all the embarrassing anecdotes her mother would be telling the older children about her. In a way, it was worse to wonder what she would be saying than to hear it. She always kept to herself during church activities because she felt the other children could not possibly like her after hearing her mother's stories about her.

After suffering through an hour of Sunday school, Bristol had to sit through another hour of church for the worship service. She always found herself between her mother and her sister. "You really can't sing, can you," her mother would whisper to Bristol after a hymn sung by the congregation. Her mother whispered to both her girls throughout the service. She would point out someone's hat as being ugly, something she would never wear, or that someone's dress had too loud a pattern, or did you know Mrs. Someone Else had just taken a trip to Europe, wonder where she gets all her money, aren't the altar flowers extra beautiful, maybe someone else ordered them this time instead of the church secretary, look at the high heels That One is wearing, how can she walk. Bristol wondered why her mother felt she could criticize the women of the church for the way they dressed when her own daughter had to wear ill-fitting hand-me-downs. Sometimes Lucy would whisper, "Shhhhh," and her mother would then write notes on the church bulletin. She showed them first to Bristol to read, then would reach across her for Lucy to read.

On the way home one Sunday after Bristol whispered back, "Don't throw stones if you live in a glass house," her mother played what Bristol and Lucy referred to as their mother's Poor Me game, this time for the benefit of their father.

In a choking voice, Elizabeth whined about how bad Bristol made her feel with that comment in church. "How could she say something like that to me? That was so mean to insinuate that there's something wrong with me."

"Bristol," Elizabeth turned to her daughter in the back seat, "how can you feel your mother is offensive? You really hurt me." She sniffed and used a tissue on her eyes. "I can only hope you didn't mean what you said."

The second set of Bristol's dreams was still recurring. In her childhood, Bristol was riding in a car. After learning to drive, she became the driver. In each of these dreams throughout the years, the car came to a long, steep hill. The hill became steeper as the car continued to climb, until Bristol was afraid it would tumble over backward from gravity before reaching the top. Just as the car approached the very top, there was a stop sign. Bristol knew that if the car stopped, it would definitely flip over front to rear. She either woke at this point, or the dream ended, and she continued in a fitful sleep.

Young Bristol tried hard to do what was expected of her. She listened to her parents and to her teachers, yet it seemed she could never live up to her mother's expectations. Elizabeth frequently pointed out the accomplishments of the older sister while tending to be critical of Bristol. "You're so thin, Bristol, straight as a stick. Turn sideways and you'll blow away. You need to eat more if you want to have some curves like Lucy." Or "Your hair is so coarse and straight. Too bad you didn't inherit your father's curly hair like Lucy." Or "You're so awkward, Bristol. We'll have to find you some finishing lessons for you to learn some grace."

Her father was the champion of both Bristol and Lucy. He told his girls they could accomplish anything they wanted and become whatever they wanted. Bristol hung onto his words of praise and encouragement. Her low self-esteem came from her mother, who constantly made her feel self-conscious, insecure, and unworthy, but her father gave her hope.

Bristol adored her father. That made it even more painful on the many occasions she overheard her mother reporting lies to her father. Bristol and Lucy would be in bed for two or three hours before their parents came upstairs. The sounds of them preparing for bed would wake Bristol. She would roll over and try to go back to sleep, but when her parents began softly talking in the room next to hers, she could overhear.

"How was your day, Lizzy?" her father would ask.

Elizabeth would answer with something like, "Oh, it would have been a pretty good day. Lucy brought home an A on her spelling test. But I sure do miss my sister, and Bristol really ruined it when she got smart-mouthed with me. She never does what I ask of her. She's no help to me at all." Her parents would continue to speak softly, and Bristol would only catch phrases here and there. She heard enough for her to realize her mother was making things up. It always began with a short comment praising Lucy before evolving into a list of imagined offenses against Bristol.

Bristol, horrified that her father was hearing these lies, wanted to jump out of bed and run into her parents' bedroom to proclaim her innocence. The thought of being in trouble for eavesdropping held her back. She did not want her father to believe the falsehoods. Unable to confront her accuser, she would cry silent tears until her parents quit talking and she fell asleep.

Sometimes Bristol would overhear her mother talking long distance with her sister Kay in Ohio. It was always the Poor Me game. Elizabeth would go down a list of complaints usually including a headache, living too far from her sister and missing her, and that she could not keep the house straight because her girls messed it up. "Someday they'll move out, and then I'll be able to keep it clean." Bristol wondered how she could say that when it was their mother's own clutter strewn around the house, along with the messes from Elizabeth's various projects she worked on for her organizations. Bristol and Lucy kept their personal belongings in their rooms to protect them from becoming lost in the disorder.

Elizabeth and Kay had always been close. They grew up in Asheville, North Carolina. When Kay met Dean Collier while he was on vacation in Asheville, a whirlwind romance led to a long-distance romance when Dean went back home to Akron, Ohio. Three years and six visits back and forth later, Kay and Dean married and Kay moved to Ohio. Elizabeth moaned about the loss of her sister ever since, and she talked to Kay on the phone several hours a week.

Sometimes her mother would be having coffee with one of the neighbors, or talking on the phone with her sister, and forget to meet the girls' school bus. They scampered into the house, ready to share their day with their mother who was not there for them.

During Bristol's fifth grade year, her family moved from North Carolina to Ohio when her father accepted a job working at the Goodyear Tire and Rubber Company so Elizabeth could be near her dear Kay.

Lester took his entire family to Akron when he first interviewed for the job. They stayed with Kay and Dean. About one in the morning on the first night of their four-day visit, the house was quiet and dark. Everyone was sound asleep except for Dean Collier.

Uncle Dean crept quietly into the living room where Bristol slept on the couch and Lucy slept on a cot.

Bristol was dreaming that her family's car was nearing the top of the nearly vertical hill. When the stop sign appeared and the car began to tilt over backward, she woke. "What the …"

Uncle Dean was bending over her as she lay on the couch. The covers were down around her knees. Uncle Dean had the elastic of her panties in one hand, a flashlight in the other. "What are you doing?" she finally got out as the elastic snapped back in place at her waist.

"Just checkin' on you. You were uncovered." He pulled the blankets up to Bristol's shoulders. "Shh. Go back to sleep."

Bristol gripped the covers tightly and watched her uncle skulk toward the bedrooms. She was horrified. What had he been doing? What had he seen? Did he touch her, or was she awake in time? Did he touch Lucy, too? Did Lucy know? Should she wake her up and find out or warn her? What will their parents do? How could she even tell her father? Maybe she would just tell her mother and Lucy in the morning. Their family would have to stay in a hotel for the rest of the trip. Surely her parents wouldn't make her stay here another night.

Bristol fretted the rest of the night, afraid to go back to sleep or to let go of the covers clutched tightly in her hands. Her eyes flew open at each creak and groan of the house until she was sure it was not Uncle Dean returning.

At first light, Bristol jumped up to use the bathroom. She locked the door. She took a long, hot shower to wash off the dirty feeling that her Uncle Dean gave her. As she lathered and scrubbed, she wondered how she would deal with this situation. She hated the thought of having to face her uncle this morning. How would he react? How would she? How should she react?

She dried off and slowly dressed, procrastinating. Finally, unlocking the door, she peaked out to be sure her uncle was not lurking nearby. She dashed into the bedroom where her parents slept. The bed was made and they were not there.

Smelling coffee, she followed her nose. Lucy was in the living room, folding her blankets, still in her pajamas. Bristol continued into the kitchen.

"You're finished in the bathroom?" her father asked. Bristol nodded. "All right, then. It's my turn." He left the room.

"It's about time you finished," her mother scolded. "There's only one bathroom in this house, you know. Other people live here, too. Did you leave any hot water?"

"Oh, Mom, I have something to tell you. Can you sit down?"

Elizabeth reached into the cupboard for the coffee mugs and continued moving about the kitchen. "I thought I'd start coffee and lay out the breakfast before everyone's up."

"Mom, please sit down."

"Just tell me. I can listen while I work."

"Please sit down and listen. This is important."

"Go on." Her mother continued moving around the kitchen.

Bristol gave up having her mother's full attention. She massaged her temples, then looked over her shoulder to make sure no one else was in earshot. "Mom, it's Uncle Dean. Did you, uh, did you know that, uh, that there's something funny about him?"

Elizabeth poured milk into the pitcher that matched Aunt Kay's sugar bowl and set them both on the table. She turned to the cupboard for cereal bowls. "Funny? You mean humorous?"

"No, Mom. I mean off, as in way off, as in weird."

"Bristol! Don't talk like that! We're in their home. Be nice." She set the bowls on the table and turned to the refrigerator for orange juice.

"You don't understand. It's Uncle Dean who isn't nice. He's weird, as in a pervert."

Elizabeth shrank back against the counter and wrapped her arms around herself. "You watch your mouth!"

They both looked to be sure no one else was near. Bristol slumped onto a kitchen chair. She folded her arms across her chest, partly in anger at her mother's response, and partly subconsciously protecting herself.

"But Mom, in the middle of the night, he came into the living room and pulled off my covers, and he pulled my pants down! He had a flashlight and he was looking at me!"

Elizabeth's hand flew to her mouth as Bristol continued. "I can't stay here again. We have to go to a hotel or something for the rest of the trip. Or go back home. Can we just go home?"

Elizabeth sank onto a kitchen chair. "But Bristol, you must have been dreaming, or you misinterpreted what happened. Surely, my sister's husband, your Uncle Dean, is not a pedophile or a pervert! You keep quiet about this," she hissed.

"There's no other way to interpret this. He did what he did. I can't sleep here again. Don't make me." Bristol pleaded. "He might come out at night again and try something." She twisted a lock of her hair, willing her mother to take her part.

"Let me speak with Lucy about this, then I'll see what your father says. "I'll get back to you."

Bristol hurried to the living room to ask Lucy to speak with their mother before the rest of the family was around. Both girls entered the kitchen.

"Good morning, Pumpkin!" Elizabeth greeted Lucy warmly. Giving Bristol a frowning glance, she asked Lucy, "Did you sleep well?"

"Yeah, OK. So, what's up? Why the meeting?"

Bristol explained the night's event. "Did he wake you up, too, Lucy? Or did I scare him off before he got around to you?"

Lucy frowned at her sister. "I never heard him in the night. Are you sure you weren't dreaming?"

"No, I wasn't dreaming, and I don't want to stay here another night."

"Hush, child, here come Aunt Kay and Uncle Dean. Not

another word about this," their mother admonished. She busied herself pouring coffee.

The rest of the day visiting the sites in Akron was long and slow. She wondered when her mother would have time to speak privately with her father.

Back in her aunt and uncle's house late that afternoon, Bristol cornered her mother. "What did Dad say? Can we go to a hotel tonight?"

"Hush! Someone will hear you! No, we can't go to a hotel. What would the family think about us changing our plans?"

"Can't we tell them why? Tell them about Uncle Dean?"

"No! Don't say a word. Don't make waves. Go on now."

"Well, then can I sleep in your room with you?"

"Of course not. The couch isn't big enough for your father. How silly of you. Now hush! We're not changing the sleeping arrangements. What would they think?" With that, Elizabeth walked away.

Bristol wondered how her mother could rate how it would look to the family over the safety of her two daughters.

...

Bristol was nervous about starting in her new Ohio school for the rest of fifth grade. She wanted desperately to fit in. The children in her old school in North Carolina tended to dislike her. She had made fun of others as she tried to compensate for her lack of fashionable clothes and for her lack of the best grades. In return, she was ignored at recess, the last to be chosen for a sports team in gym class, and never invited to their lunch tables to eat or to their homes for birthday or slumber parties. She decided she would have the chance to turn things around in her new school.

Bristol waited and watched to pick out the most popular girl in the class and made a point of becoming her friend. It was Mary Beth Nicely, an attractive girl with long blond hair, blue eyes, and a petite, turned-up nose, who sat toward the back of the room. Bristol devised a plan to ask the teacher to move her seat so she could sit next to Mary Beth.

She arrived in the classroom a few minutes early the next morning to talk with her teacher alone. "Mrs. Bell, that boy Mickey, who sits behind me, keeps poking me in the back with his pencil, and he whispers naughty things to me when you turn around to write on the board."

"Oh, he does, does he?" Mrs. Bell, a seasoned teacher, did not think that was the case, but she wanted to hear what Bristol had to say.

"Yes, and I think you should change my seat so I don't have to put up with him. Can I sit about four seats back? I could trade with Jimmy. He's friends with Mickey, so they would get along OK, and there wouldn't be any more problems."

"Does Mickey hurt you with the pencil?"

"Uh, no, he must use the eraser end." Bristol did not want Mickey to be in trouble because he would tell Mrs. Bell this was not true.

"What kind of things does he whisper to you?"

"Well, I can't really tell you. It's embarrassing. Will you please just change my seat?"

Mrs. Bell decided to allow this to play out even though she did not know the real reason for the request. She wanted the new girl to have every chance of succeeding in her new environment. "Umm. I think we could try this out. Here comes Jimmy."

The children were filing into the classroom, tossing book bags and jackets, and taking their seats. Mrs. Bell asked to speak with Jimmy. "Jimmy, I can change your seat closer to the front." Jimmy frowned until Mrs. Bell continued. "Would you like to sit behind your friend Mickey?

Now smiling, he answered, "Yeah, can I sit there now?"

"Yes, you may, on a trial period. If you and Mickey behave yourselves, perhaps you can sit there more permanently."

With her seat now beside Mary Beth, Bristol began a campaign to become her friend. She passed her notes that complimented her or that made fun of one of the other children who were not in Mary Beth's in-group. During recess and gym class, Bristol maneuvered to be next to Mary Beth and her friends. She sat with them at their lunch table, uninvited, but as though she was a part of their group. No one challenged her, and she became a defacto member during fifth and sixth grades.

...

Three grade schools sent their students to the one junior high in the district for seventh, eighth, and ninth grades. This was a much larger student body than her elementary school, and instead of having the same classmates all day, Bristol found many different students in each of her classes. She waited and observed. Although well liked, it seemed her friend Mary Beth was no longer the most popular girl in the school.

Barbara Ann Nims seemed to be the most popular, plus she was in Girl Scouts, a group that sounded fun. They went tent camping and swimming in the summers, and spent some weekends in a cabin at Camp Ledgewood during the winter. They hiked, made s'mores, earned badges, acted in skits, and had all kinds of fun. Many of the other popular girls were in the scouting program with Barbara.

The problem was Barbara and Mary Beth were not friends. Bristol asked Barbara why not.

"Because Mary Beth had a slumber party and didn't invite me, but I don't need her. I have lots of fun she isn't part of."

Bristol was curious. "Didn't you just meet her when school started this fall? Did she know you when she had the party?"

"Oh, yeah, she knew me. We go to the same church. We're in a Sunday school class together."

Bristol wanted to be part of the fun with Barbara. She stopped hanging around Mary Beth and waited for an opportunity. It came during a bonfire pep rally for the school's football team. Many of the students had brought marshmallow roasting forks and were toasting or burning marshmallows over the fire. Bristol pulled her marshmallows out of the flames, blew the fire out, and stepped back without looking. She inadvertently backed into the prong of the long-handled fork another student held in front of himself.

Startled, she jumped, and as she turned around, she saw a large-eared boy with a surprised expression. She cried out, "You burned me! What the heck are you doing, Dumbo? You should watch it."

"I'm sorry," the student apologized, "but you backed into me. *You* should watch it. Are you OK?"

"Of course, I'm OK," Bristol snapped and walked away to search for Barbara. When she found her, she exclaimed, not caring who else would hear, "Look, Barbara, Mary Beth stabbed me with her fork, and it was hot from the fire."

Bristol pulled her shirt part way out of her jeans to have Barbara check the small wound on her lower back. Others glanced at it, too, and wondered why Mary Beth would do such a thing.

"Your shirt has a small burn hole in it, too," Barbara told her. "Don't worry; you don't need her in your life. I found that out. Hey, why don't you come to the next Girl Scout meeting with us? We meet in room 202 every Tuesday, right after the last class. Come on. You'll really like it."

Bristol pretended to consider the offer before agreeing to be there.

...

During the summer between her seventh and eighth grade years, the Jameses sent Bristol and Lucy to one week of summer camp. Both girls begged their mother to leave church as soon as the service ended so they could arrive at the camp in time to claim a top bunk. Elizabeth agreed, but the family waited in the car for forty minutes while Elizabeth talked to her church friends. By the time they drove home, had dinner, and finally arrived at the camp, all the top bunks were taken. Both girls were disappointed.

They did have fun that week swimming and riding horses. Bristol tried to make friends by telling the other girls she had a horse of her own at home. She hoped Lucy would not hear about it and give her away. It was working for her because two of the horse-crazy girls befriended her. They kept asking about her horse and whether they could come to visit after camp. Bristol would not commit.

In eighth grade, Bristol decided to try out for the lead in the school play. Mr. Ealey, the English teacher, was their drama coach. He posted the chosen cast members on the bulletin board in the main hallway. He cast Bristol for a small part with a few short lines in the first act. When Bristol saw she made a part in the play, she was thrilled until she realized how small the part was.

That evening at home she told her parents. Lester smiled and was pleased for her. "Good for you, Honey. You should have fun with the other cast members. Put the performance date on the calendar and we'll all be there to watch you."

Her mother wanted to know, "How big a part is it? Did you get the lead? I'll tell my friends so they can come watch my daughter in the school play."

"Well, no, I'm in the first act." Bristol did not mention she was only in one scene.

When her mother responded, "Oh," without saying anything more, Bristol decided not to accept the part. After thinking it over for a day, she decided maybe she did still want to be part of the camaraderie of the drama club.

Still conflicted, she turned up for the first play practice held in the band room. Mr. Ealey wanted to work with the principal actors first. He sent other groups of actors to the three soundproof practice rooms to rehearse their lines.

Bristol was sitting in practice room one with the other girl in her scene. Christy leafed through her play script. "We come in at the beginning of scene II. It's on page 31. Want to read through it?"

In response, Bristol began a tirade in an angry outburst. "I'm not sure I want this stupid part. I'm better than a two-bit player." Her voice rose as she continued ranting. "These parts are so small we hardly need to go over these stupid lines."

Christy, astonished, did not respond as Bristol raged on. "I tried out for the lead character, and Mr. Ealey gives me this one-scene part so small it doesn't even have a name, just Waitress One. He should at least have given me the part of …"

She was interrupted by Mr. Ealey, who heard the shouting even though the practice room was soundproofed. He jerked the door open and grabbed Christy by the arm. He yanked her from her seat and told her to pick up her things and leave.

"But, but, I didn't say anything. It wasn't me," Christy protested.

"Out!" Mr. Ealey pointed to the door. Bristol suddenly decided she did, after all, want to be in the play, and she certainly did not want to be in trouble for shouting and carrying on. She sat quietly in her chair, ankles crossed, hands clasped in her lap, looking demurely at the floor.

"No, Mr. Ealey, really, it wasn't me," Christy insisted. She looked at Bristol, expecting confirmation of the truth, but Bristol kept quiet and allowed the crisis to play out.

"Out! Now!" Ealey pointed at the door.

Christy threw the play script onto the chair and grabbed her purse and book bag. She shouldered her way past Ealey and stormed out the door in a huff.

The night of the performance, Bristol walked to the school. Her father was sick and would not be coming. Her mother was to arrive shortly before curtain time. She would drive Bristol home.

Her mother never showed. After the last curtain call, Bristol searched the now brightly lit auditorium for her mother. Finally, she gave up and walked home in the dark.

Her mother was sitting in the living room. "How did it go?" she asked Bristol.

"If you had been there, you would know. Where were you?" Bristol demanded, slamming her purse onto the end table.

"My sister asked me to come over to help her with a problem she had sewing this new dress pattern. I guess I kind of forgot. We worked her problem out, though."

As if this excused her, Bristol thought.

"I had to walk home almost two miles in the dark." Secretly Bristol was glad her mother had not seen the play and was not aware of how small the part was.

"I would have been there, but Kay needed me. Didn't you have any friends you could have walked home with? I know you're not real popular, but wasn't someone available?"

Elizabeth was frequently late to pick up the girls from the school bus, or from the appointed time after shopping at the mall, or from their jobs when they were older. When she turned sixteen, Bristol worked at a small boutique in a strip mall between a state store selling alcohol and a bar. The store closed at nine o'clock. Her mother was to pick her up at nine-ten, giving her time to count out her money drawer. The other employees would hurry off into the night, leaving Bristol standing outside the now locked store as she waited for her ride home. Men would whistle at her as they came and went from the liquor store or the bar. When her mother arrived, sometimes as much as an hour late, Bristol would explain how unsafe she felt.

Elizabeth was never sympathetic and never apologized. She watched her daughter buckle her seat belt and justified, "I'm sure you were safe enough. Nothing is going to happen to you. Kay was telling me something, and I lost track of the time. You're going home now, so don't sweat it."

Then Elizabeth redirected, "And what, you're a small store clerk. You can't be that all your life. Where are you going from here? Can you at least become the store manager or better yet, a district manager? I want to be proud of my daughter."

Yup, Mom's sister always comes first, then her friends, then her own family last. And there she goes again turning things around from her to me and what I should do or be. Bristol was furious, but she was learning from her mother how to put a spin on the topic at hand, and how to deflect offensive comments by putting the other person on the defense.

"Geez, Mom, I'm only sixteen. This is just a part-time job until I go to college for a real career."

"Well, you better decide what it is you want to do without going to college, because with paying for your sister now, we can't afford it for you. If you really want to go, although I think with your grades it would be a waste of time and money, but if you really want to go, you'll have to pay for it yourself, so save your money and apply for grants." Elizabeth turned into their driveway and Bristol blinked away tears.

...

Bristol went through high school testing her skills of spin and manipulation. When the Girl Scout troop began having too many winter camp outs to suit Bristol, she dumped Barbara Ann

Nims' friendship for one with Linda Bains, who was captain of the cheerleading squad. She decided that Linda, being a cheerleader, was more popular than Barbara, and she would rather be a cheerleader than a Girl Scout.

Linda and her cheerleader friends taught Bristol the cheers during their practice sessions so Bristol would be prepared to try out for next year's squad. Bristol did not make it. The girls ended the friendship with Bristol to become friends with the three new squad members. While looking for another group to join, Bristol gossiped about the whole cheerleading squad. Only some of what she said was true.

She would decide on a group, find the leader of that group, court a friendship with that leader, and worm her way into the group. The friendships tended to last only a few months when either she would decide to move on to another group more to her liking, or the group would freeze her out. She was building a reputation for being able to have only one friend at a time, for searching out the leader or most popular person in a group, then manipulating others away from that leader while she cozied up to them. She graduated from high school with no friends.

At the dinner table early that summer after graduation, Bristol asked her parents to buy her a car. "I need to find a better job, so I'll be driving to a bunch of interviews. I'll probably not find anything around here, so that means driving to Akron every day. It doesn't have to be a new car, just reliable."

Her father agreed, "We can look around and see what we can find."

Her mother was not as agreeable. "We just bought your sister a car for her college graduation. It'll be difficult to come up with the money right now. Anyway, you have your savings account from your part-time job. Use that." Elizabeth picked up the platter of burned, dried-up pork chops.

"Does anyone want another pork chop?" No one did.

Bristol set down her fork and put her fists on the table, one on each side of her plate. "Mom, you paid for her college and bought her a car. You refuse to pay for me to go to school, and now you don't want to buy me a car, either. Why can't you do for me what you do for her?" The unequal treatment her mother gave her two daughters always hurt Bristol. She resented the offenses, became both frustrated and outraged when she was confronted with them, and her self-esteem suffered.

"Now Bristol, it isn't because we don't want to do for you. You have to understand there is only so much money. You can't do everything you want, and you can't have everything you want," Elizabeth told her. "Count your blessings. We don't charge you room and board, even though you've graduated from high school."

Bristol looked at her father, but he kept eating and did not say anything.

"Mom, you should be happy to buy me a car so you don't have to drive me to and from work at the boutique anymore. And you'll have to drive me to my job interviews, too, if I don't have my own car. Come on."

"Bristol," her father responded, "we can go out Saturday to look around the car lots."

"OK, Dad!" Bristol was pleased at this new development in the right direction. "I work until three. Can you pick me up at the store and we'll go look?"

"Yes, we'll do it." He smiled at his daughter.

Bristol knew her father, unlike her mother, was as good as his word. That meant she would be car shopping Saturday. Even if she had to spend her own money toward a car, if her father helped, too, soon she would have her freedom and not have to wait on her mother.

The car shopping was a success. Her father helped her with a down payment and co-signed for a loan on a five-year-old compact with newer tires and no rust. Bristol did not have to use any of her savings. With her own money, she bought two stylish business suits using her discount at the boutique. She added five blouses of assorted colors to change the look. Each was low-cut enough to show herself off while remaining in the realm of good taste for business. These would be suitable for job interviews and, hopefully, for her new job.

Her tenth job interview was with a Larry Brown from an accounting firm that managed payroll, taxes, and bookkeeping. They also had a financial planning department. The job opening was for a receptionist. It did not require education after a high school diploma.

Bristol sat across from Mr. Brown, answering his questions as he looked over her application. She sat forward as though listening to him intently, while showing her cleavage to its best advantage. "Yes, I worked at the boutique all through high school. I still work there now. It has given me so much experience working with the public, even the angry public. I've had to smooth ruffled feathers from time to time to keep customers happy. I do scheduling, answer the phone, stock work, sales, whatever is needed. My cash drawer always comes out even."

Brown called her back three days later with a job offer that Bristol accepted happily. When she told her parents, her father congratulated her. Her mother asked her where she could go from there.

Bristol's skills served her well to play the game of office politics to influence her boss and maneuver to a better position within the company. She joined the company bowling league where she could overhear conversations about the other employees and about the company itself. Knowledge could be useful. When she learned one of the women was looking for another job, she shared the information with Mr. Brown, who thanked Bristol and promptly fired the woman. When one of the men joked with another how he buried a mistake in the middle of a lengthy report, they chuckled. Bristol found it the next day and showed it to Mr. Brown. He thanked her and took her to lunch. As she continued to report to him, he began to take her to lunch weekly.

When an angry client called, she would appease them by telling them what they wanted to hear, even if she had to make up something. "Yes, Mr. Smith. We are well aware you need that report by next week. One of the accountants is working on it as we speak. Don't you worry. It will be ready on time." She pulled Mr. Smith's file and placed it on the top of the accountant's in-basket.

"Yes, Mrs. Jones, the very best accountant in the firm is handling it for you. Don't worry." *Whoever. Whatever.*

Bristol always let Mr. Brown know when she appeased a client. Without giving him details, she let him know when she finished work before a deadline. She let him know when she helped one of the secretaries with her work load, exaggerating her part.

Within a year, Mr. Brown's secretary left the firm. Bristol immediately applied for the job and began to sell herself to Mr. Brown. "I know more about our company than anyone you could hire from outside," she reasoned. "I've already been doing so much of her work, I'm ready to step into her position. I've already proven my loyalty to you. I could prove to be even more valuable to you as your secretary."

Mr. Brown was not sure how that could be, but he promoted Bristol to secretary and gave her the accompanying pay raise. Her mother told her, "Good for you, but is this as high as you can go?"

Bristol already had her eye on the position of assistant office manager. She began dating an accountant and asked him to teach her the payroll system. Then she asked him to show her how to use the spreadsheets on the computer. She watched as he typed in his password to open the program. She made a mental note of the password. He taught her how to use the Quicken computer program, billing, accounts payable, and payroll for outside companies.

When the position of assistant office manager became open fifteen months later, Bristol was ready. She applied for the job, interviewed for it with Mr. Brown, demonstrated her knowledge of the work, and was promoted with another pay increase. She broke up with the accountant.

She was one step from her top goal of office manager. Gloria Holms was the present office manager. Bristol schmoozed her into a friendship. They went to lunch together several times a week, and Bristol would telephone her at night to gossip about the other employees. During the day, Bristol took on more of Gloria's duties in the guise of helping her. She was ready to take her job.

When Gloria gave Bristol mistakes to correct, Bristol first took them to Mr. Brown. She told him the mistakes were made by Gloria, but that Bristol found them and would correct them.

Reports that Gloria wrote without her name on them, Bristol showed to Mr. Brown and told him she herself wrote them. When Gloria shared an idea with Bristol, Bristol would share it with Mr. Brown as though it were her own idea. Finally, Bristol made a list of the job duties of the assistant office manager and the office manager. She showed it to Mr. Brown.

"You know, I'm doing all these, don't you? And I'm correcting Gloria's mistakes. It's fortunate I'm finding them. The thing is, it's like Gloria's the assistant, and I'm the manager. Yet, Gloria has the title and the pay."

"Let me think about it, Bristol," Mr. Brown responded while looking at her cleavage.

Two months later, Gloria was gone and Bristol was the office manager. Her mother commented, "That's great, dear. Where can you go from there?"

Her mother's words stung. "Geez, Mom, I'm only twenty-one and I'm the office manager of a large firm. You should be proud of me."

Elizabeth did not relent. "Well, you know, onward and upward."

Bristol left the room for her own bedroom to hide her tears. *It's never enough.*

...

Lucy James had graduated from college, found a job, and moved out of the family home by the time Bristol was twenty-two. Bristol continued to live with her parents and save her money. She gave them a small amount to pay for groceries and to help with household expenses, but she was able to save most of her income, which was the only reason she still lived at home.

Her mother was a constant irritant, always criticizing her.

One evening at dinner, her mother pointed out, "Bristol, you've finally gained some weight, but you're overdoing it now. You're getting a bit chunky. Better cut down." She handed Bristol the bowl of mashed potatoes.

Bristol considered the bowl, wanting another serving, but she passed the bowl to her father without taking another helping.

"Why don't you let me cut your hair after dinner?" her mother asked her. "It's getting too long. You have frizzy, split ends. Anyone want more fish sticks?" Elizabeth picked up the platter.

Bristol hated fish sticks that came frozen from the store, but her mother made them once a week. She also hated chewy, gristly, minute steaks which Elizabeth served weekly. "No, I'll pass. Dad?"

Her father finished off the fish sticks. *Probably out of hunger, not because he likes them,* Bristol thought. Her father did not allow his girls to criticize the meals. He told them their mother worked hard to prepare meals, and they should eat what they were given. *Like she really works hard, throwing frozen food in pans, then reading the newspaper in the living room until she smells something burning.*

"What about your hair? Want me to trim it for you?"

"No thanks, Mom. I'll get it done at the beauty shop. I have a girl I like who does it now." Bristol was trying to grow it long. Every time her mother agreed to trim just the split ends, her hair ended up in a short cut again. Bristol could not trust her.

"You might like her, but she isn't doing you any justice. Just look at that frizz. Those ends need cut."

Bristol wished her mother would shut up. She changed the subject. "You're going to have a big five-o birthday in three months, Mom. How do you want to celebrate?" She eyed the chocolate cake her mother was handing out, but she refused reluctantly. "No, thank you."

"It's delicious. Better have some," her mother persuaded.

"No, I'm full," Bristol lied to cover up her longing. She knew she was about fifteen pounds overweight. Elizabeth kept disapproving of her weight gain while simultaneously encouraging her to eat fattening foods.

"So, I was talking to Lucy and Dad, and we think you should celebrate in a bigger than usual way. We want to do something like a dinner in an upscale restaurant with all of us and Aunt Kay and uh, I guess Uncle Dean." Bristol nearly choked as she said Dean's name.

"No, that's not what I want."

"What do you want, then? We want to have time to plan it." Bristol and Lucy did not want the pressure of last minute planning.

"Well, I don't know, yet. Something nice. I'll let you know when I think of something. How about clearing the table and putting the leftover food away for me. I'm going to sit down and finish reading the paper."

Lucy talked to Elizabeth on the phone regularly and frequently asked what kind of celebration their mother wanted for her fiftieth birthday. Bristol asked during dinner with her parents most evenings. Elizabeth never had an answer, and she turned down all suggestions. Her birthday was now a month away.

"We could rent a limousine, pick up Aunt Kay and Uncle Dean, then go to a fancy restaurant. If we have more time on the limousine service, we could drive around for awhile after dinner. That would be kind of fun," Bristol suggested.

"No, I don't want to do that," her mother responded as usual.

"How about dinner, then a movie of your choice, and ice cream after? Or we could celebrate at the church on the Sunday before and invite everyone to the social hall for ice cream and cake."

"No, I don't think so."

Bristol was frustrated. "What do you want, then? Tell us so we can plan!"

"I don't know. I'll think about it. But here's something I want you to think about. What are you doing tomorrow night?"

Bristol sighed, knowing her plans to relax were about to change. "Nothing, Mom, absolutely nothing. This has been a really hard week at work, and I want to come home, relax, and go to bed early. I'm really tired, and I still have tomorrow left in the work week." She was afraid to ask why, but her mother continued.

"I want you to go with me to the Carousel Dinner Theatre tomorrow night to see that new show that's supposed to be so good. Will you go with me?"

"Oh, man, no. Do you have tickets or were you going to buy them at the door? I mean, I really don't want to go. Can't you have Dad go with you?" Bristol rubbed her tired eyes hoping, the tickets had not yet been purchased.

"Your father doesn't enjoy going to the theatre. I know he'll say no. Come on. If you don't go, I can't go, and I already have the tickets. You won't have to pay anything," Elizabeth coaxed.

"Mom, please. I really don't want to go. Why didn't you ask me before you bought the tickets? I could maybe go another night, but I've just been so tired this week with the daylight savings time change and the heavy load at work. Just ask Dad. He might surprise you and go."

"Well, I did ask him, and he declined. Come on and go with me so I can go," Elizabeth wheedled.

"Tell you what, Mom. I really don't want to go. But, if you call Lucy and Aunt Kay to see if one of them will go with you, if they can't, then I'll go just so you don't waste the money."

"OK, I'll call them." Elizabeth went into the living room to make her calls. Bristol went upstairs to her room.

It was only ten minutes when Elizabeth knocked on Bristol's bedroom door. "Can I come in?"

"Yeah, come on," Bristol sighed, resigned. "Did you reach them?"

"I did, and neither of them can go. You can go there straight from work. We can meet in the lobby. Be there by five-thirty." Elizabeth left the room before Bristol could refuse.

The next evening Bristol had a difficult time driving from work to the dinner theatre. She fought sleep and wished she could go home and go to bed. *This is going to be a long night!* She made it to the theatre first and sat on a bench waiting for her mother to join her.

When her mother finally arrived forty-five minutes later, she trooped in the door with twenty of her friends from her lodge, looked around, and spotted her daughter sitting on the bench. She left her cortege of friends and went to her daughter. "There you are! Were you waiting long?" Elizabeth inquired pleasantly as though nothing were wrong.

"Yes, I have!" Bristol snarled quietly, not wanting others to hear her anger at her mother. "You told me five-thirty! It's six-fifteen! What a manipulator you are!"

"What?"

"Well, you said you couldn't come unless I came with you, but you have all these friends with you. You could have come! You're with them. You made me come here under false pretenses. This isn't right! You knew I didn't want to come. I should just go home right now!" Bristol would have stood up, but she thought she just might be tempted to hit her mother if they were face-to-face. Bristol was tempted to leave, but she worried what her mother would tell her friends about her if she left. *She'll tell them what a terrible daughter I am, that I picked a fight with her, got mad and left or something. Anyway, she already bought the tickets and they're expensive. This better be entertaining or I'll be asleep at the table.*

She was right. After a heavy steak dinner, the curtain opened, and the show began. The loud music and good story line was not enough to keep Bristol's eyes from closing as she cradled her head against her hand, elbow on the table.

This was not the last straw for Bristol in her relationship with her mother. This was just another in a series of episodes occurring during her whole life.

The last straw, the one that made Bristol decide to move out, was connected to her mother's fiftieth birthday party.

Lucy and Bristol confronted Elizabeth together in front of

their father. Lucy had joined the rest of the family for dinner that evening. After dessert, Lucy chided, “Mom, we have been begging you to tell us how you want to celebrate your birthday, and you keep putting off telling us what you want.”

“Yeah, Mom,” Bristol chimed in. “Now doors of opportunity have closed because it’s too late. So, what do you want? If you can’t tell us tonight, we’re going to plan something and surprise you.”

“I want all my friends to come,” Elizabeth answered.

Bristol and Lucy looked at each other and groaned. “What do you mean by all your friends?” Lucy asked for both of them.

“Well, I mean all of them. My neighbors, my church friends, my friends from lodge and bowling, oh, and the card club members. All my friends, and my family, too, and Dad’s family because they’re my family, too. I couldn’t leave anyone out.”

“Mom, it’s just two weeks away. How do you expect us to plan something that big in that short of time?” Bristol demanded. Most of your family lives in North Carolina. Your cousins would need more time to plan to come up here.”

“I don’t know,” Elizabeth whispered, as though it did not matter because it was up to her daughters, not up to her.

“Dad?” Lucy asked for help, but none was forthcoming.

“Just do the best you can, girls,” their father advised.

“Mom, we’ll give you a party. It will be on Sunday after your birthday on Saturday. Find a dress to wear.” Lucy slapped the kitchen table and stood to leave. “Bristol, come over after work tomorrow and we’ll plan. If you have a chance before then, make some notes of some ideas. I have a few.” Lucy bid her good-byes and left.

As Bristol sat in Lucy's living room working out details of the party, Lucy's phone rang. It was Aunt Kay. When Kay learned Bristol was there, too, she asked to be put on speaker phone.

"You two girls should be ashamed of yourselves," Kay began. "This is a big mile-stone birthday for your mother. You should have planned something extra special for her. She called me crying that her girls aren't doing anything for her. Did you forget it was her birthday?"

"Good grief!" Bristol groaned, rolling her eyes at Lucy.

"Aunt Kay," Lucy spoke into the phone, "we have been begging our mother for three months to tell us what she wants for her birthday to be special. She kept putting us off. Finally, just last night we told her we're going ahead to plan a party. That's what we're doing tonight. So why is she telling you we aren't doing anything when she knows good and well we are, and we've been trying to for three months?" Lucy was trying not to yell at Aunt Kay.

Kay settled down, and after a pause acknowledged, "I don't know, Honey. I guess she was just playing Poor Me the way she does."

"Gee, Aunt Kay, that's what we call it, too. So, you know she does that. We always figured you believed everything she said." Lucy sat down on her armchair with this revelation.

"No, Honey. I've known your mother all my life, remember. You could say I know what she's like. I understand you two girls have a challenging time dealing with her, but she loves you. You have to appreciate that."

Bristol and Lucy made the party plans that evening. The next day, Molly McKnight, the woman in charge of the church circle, called Bristol. She asked if the circle could provide a birthday celebration for Elizabeth after church on the Sunday of her birthday weekend, since her family was not giving her one this year. Bristol explained she and Lucy were planning to give their mother a birthday party on that very day and intended to give an open invitation to the entire church. Bristol could tell the lady was not convinced the girls were already planning a party.

Bristol phoned Lucy to tell her about Molly's call. "Geez, Lucy, she just throws us under the bus, making her own daughters look bad just to play Poor Me so people feel sorry for her."

"Oh, I don't think Mom looks at it as making us look bad. No, I don't think she means to do that. I think it just happens when she plays Poor Me for whatever gratification she gets from the sympathy."

"I think I've had all I can take. I'm going to move out." Bristol had been thinking about moving for a month or two.

"I wondered how long you were going to last living at home. Obviously, I moved out sooner than you did. I highly recommend it. You should have plenty of money saved up by now."

...

Bristol worked out a budget to determine how much rent she could afford. She found a small two-bedroom apartment twenty minutes from her job and moved from her parents' home.

This will be great, she thought. *No one to harass me.* While this was true, Bristol did discover she felt lonesome. She thought of herself as her own best company, but she was not an introvert.

She craved friendship, but she had no friends. She realized the people at work did not like her even though she had no comprehension of why. Most of the people in her church were older, and she did not care about them. The last four years of her life had been devoted to advancing her career, consequently, she had no hobbies and belonged to no clubs.

Bristol knew nothing about horses. What she did know was she needed something to make herself special in the eyes of others. She had been working and saving for four years. *If I owned my own horse, it would make me exceptional and I could make friends easier. It worked for me in summer camp.* It was time to meet some horse owners who could help her out.

Hating to appear ignorant about any subject, Bristol borrowed books on horse care from her local library. She dedicated her spare time to learning all she could about them.

She was reading about horse breeds when her mother phoned. "Bristol, why don't you come over for supper tonight. You seldom come here since you moved out. Your father and I miss you."

"Mom, it's six-thirty. I already ate supper." Bristol inserted a book mark and closed her book.

"Well, you never call or come over. You just ignore me."

Oh, boy, the Poor Me game. "I see you every Sunday in church. Anyway, it's a two-way street, Mom. You don't call me much, either, and when you do, you just complain."

"Look, Bristol, why don't you come for dinner Thursday night. In fact, why don't we set up a standing date for every Thursday? Your father would like that. I'll call Lucy and have her come, too. See you Thursday, then?"

Bristol gave a resigned sigh and agreed. "OK, Mom. What

time? What should I bring?"

"Don't bring a thing. I enjoy cooking for my girls. I'm looking forward to every Thursday now."

Bristol doubted that statement when she and Lucy arrived at their parents' home Thursday at six o'clock. Their mother was not there, and no dinner was prepared.

Lester told them he did not know they were coming. "I just made myself a sandwich. Do you want one? There's plenty of lunchmeat. Your mother went over to Aunt Kay's. I think they were going to play dominoes with Uncle Dean and a neighbor of theirs."

They visited for a while when Lester had a complaint. "Your mother told me she fell Monday and called both of you to tell you, but neither of you called her back. That's no way to treat your mother. You should have been worried about her enough to at least call her back, if not come running over to see how she was."

The sisters looked at each other. Lucy shrugged. "She didn't tell me."

Bristol rolled her eyes. "She left a message on my answering machine that only said, 'This is your mother.' But she didn't say to call her back, and she didn't say she fell. This is the first I heard of it. Did she get hurt?"

"No, nothing broken."

Partly to change the subject, Bristol brought up the idea of buying a horse. This surprised her family, but Lucy told her about a friend of hers who had a horse. "Why don't I introduce you, and you could pick her brain. She could give you the low-down about owning horses. The way she talks, they're lots of work."

"Yes, I know. But I would board and let someone else do the work. So, what's your friend's name? I'd like to talk to her."

"Geri Monarch."

...

Geri Monarch agreed to meet Bristol. They set up a time at the local Panera's.

Over soup and salad, Geri brushed her long dark hair behind her ears and asked, "So what do you want to know about horses?"

"I'm interested in buying one, so for one thing, do you know of any for sale, or where I can go to buy a good one, something exceptional?" Bristol took a drink of her Pepsi.

"I do! A member of our horse club is selling an older, well broke trail horse for a reasonable price. He's not fancy, just a plain brown, but he's safe and smooth gaited. He'd make an appropriate first horse for an inexperienced rider. Is it trail riding you want to do?"

"Yeah, I'll be trail riding, but I don't want a plain brown horse. It'll cost me just as much as owning a pretty horse, so I might as well buy a good-looking one." *Stunning is what I want.*

They both grinned.

"Well, there is truth to that, but remember, you can't ride color, or papers either. If a plain horse with no registration papers is a great trail horse that gives you a fun, safe ride, he's worth it," Geri advised.

"That reminds me," she went on. "One of our club

members, Joyce, was at a state ride with about two hundred people from all over Ohio. They had a large campfire going with a huge double circle of campers sitting all around the fire ring. It was so big that this guy talking to his buddy didn't notice Joyce and her husband sitting within hearing distance. He told his buddy he thought he saw his old horse Red he had sold two years ago. His buddy asked who had Red. He said, "That gray-haired lady that rides the ugly horse, her husband rides Red."

Geri and Bristol chuckled.

"Yeah, Joyce and Bob laughed. They were good sports about it and never let on that they heard the guy. You know, that horse was ugly. She had a massive barrel of a rib cage, and she had rubbed off her mane hair. She was bald there and had a bald spot at the top of her tail, probably from rubbing her itches. She gave Joyce an enjoyable, smooth, safe, ride, and Joyce said she only paid five hundred dollars for her."

"No way do I want someone to laugh at me because of my horse," Bristol told her. "Mine will be a good looker."

"There's a joke about that." Geri took a last bite of her salad and told the joke. "This guy goes to a farmer who had a horse for sale. The guy said he'd take the horse. The farmer said the horse didn't look so good. The guy said the horse looked good to him. The guy bought the horse but brought him back to the farmer the next day. He said the farmer sold him a blind horse. The farmer said, 'I told you he doesn't look so good.'"

They chuckled. Bristol remarked, "Yeah, I saw that one coming."

They continued to talk and laugh through dessert. Before they left, Geri invited Bristol to their next horse club meeting. Bristol agreed to be there.

...

After attending three meetings of the horse club, Bristol joined. She saw an advantage to belonging so she could have help finding a horse and eventually go on group rides. An added bonus was that Geri introduced Bristol to her brother, Richard, or Ric, as the family called him. They began dating.

Bristol found a flashy seven-year-old Arabian mare an older club member was selling because he was ready to stop trail riding after two hip replacements and two knee replacements. The horse was a handful for him, and he was afraid to ride again.

Geri advised Bristol to buy an older, calmer horse for her first horse, but Bristol thought she could handle Little Lady. Little Lady knew she could handle Bristol. After being thrown twice, Bristol sent Lady to a trainer. The trainer told Bristol she needed the training, not the horse. Bristol yanked the horse from the trainer's barn and took her back to her boarding barn. At this point, just owning a beautiful, showy horse was pleasure enough to make her feel special.

She was no longer interested in riding until Ric, who had never been interested in riding, encouraged her to try the docile horses at a livery stable. After an hour on the placid rental horses, they returned to the barn unscathed.

"See, you can do it. You just need some confidence and a quiet horse."

Instead of thanking him for encouraging her, she snapped, "I know I can do it. I just didn't want to."

Eventually, Geri talked Bristol into selling Little Lady to

buy a Tennessee Walker from another club member. Blaze was trail experienced and reliable. Bristol enjoyed riding him on the trail during a try out.

"OK, he's plain brown, but he's pretty. I mean, he has decent conformation. No one would laugh at this horse. In fact, his impeccable manners would help *you* look good. You had a great ride today. Why don't you sell Lady and buy Blaze? You can go on the club rides then. We have so much fun. Maybe later you can find your fancy dream horse."

Little Lady sold quickly and Bristol bought Blaze. With Ric's help, she bought a truck and trailer. She was set to go on the club camp outs.

...

Ric continually paid attention to Bristol and her needs. She had never experienced this much kindness and thoughtfulness. When he asked her to marry him after a year of dating, she agreed.

Her mother told her she should plan a small ceremony and pay for her wedding herself. "We can pay for a small wedding cake for you, but that's it."

Bristol was twenty-six when she married Ric in a white business suit in front of her parents, her sister Lucy, Ric's parents, and his sister Geri. They had dinner in a restaurant afterward to celebrate. The couple wanted to spend money on a home instead of a large wedding.

Although Ric was not interested in riding, he liked horses and other animals. They looked for a house with a barn so Bristol could keep her horse at home. Ric did most of the barn chores and the upkeep on their acreage. Bristol cleaned the house, managed the laundry, and kept her job as office manager. Sometimes she cooked a slapped-together meal.

Five years later, when Bristol discovered she was pregnant, Ric was overjoyed. Bristol was upset. She did not want a child who would think about her the way she thought about her own mother.

The baby was a girl. They named her Sophia after Ric's maternal grandmother. Bristol resented Sophia before she was born because she could not ride while she was pregnant. She resented her after she was born because she robbed her of so much time. She hated the stinky diapers and the baby vomit. She hated the crying and the waking up at night. She fed and changed Sophia and laid her back down. It was Ric who loved her and played with her. When he was home, he fed her and changed her diapers. Bristol was relieved to return to work after maternity leave and let the daycare handle the baby. She was happiest when Ric would baby sit and give her time to ride her horse.

Sophia grew up loved by her father and ignored by her mother. She married her high school sweetheart immediately after June graduation. Bristol was happy to have her leave home.

Bristol continued to be active with the horse club. During a club meeting, when the nominating committee reported they were unable to find anyone willing to run for the office of president, Bristol responded without waiting to be recognized. She told the group, "I'll be president. I like a challenge." *I wonder why no one on the committee asked me if I would do it?*

The current president, Kristen, asked, "Are you nominating yourself?"

"Yes, I am."

"Then we'll need a second. Anyone?"

There was silence in the room.

"Someone?"

A newer member, who did not know Bristol very well, raised her hand. "I'll second."

The nominating committee chair continued to present the slate of officers.

The president knocked her gavel once and announced they would vote on the slate as a whole since there was only one candidate per office. "We'll vote by a show of hands. How many are for?"

Most of the members raised their hand.

"Against?"

Those opposed did not raise their hand.

"This slate of officers for the coming year stands elected."

A month later, the outgoing president handed Bristol the club gavel and the notebook the club used for the protocols for its president. Bristol took the gavel, gave a sneer toward the notebook, and snipped, "I don't need that."

"But it's the guide for our club presidents to follow, including our by-laws. You need it. It will be easier to do the job if you aren't reinventing the wheel," Kristen advised.

"I know how to do the job, or I wouldn't have volunteered." Bristol turned her back and strutted away.

Several club members witnessed this exchange and shook

their heads. "Uh, oh, trouble coming," one remarked.

And trouble there was.

The club had standing committees that reported to the club board each month. Kara Leonard was the chairwoman of the trail ride committee. Bristol told her she wanted to come to the meeting when they planned the club trail rides for the year. Kara explained the president did not attend any committee meetings, that they provided written reports to everyone on the board at the board meetings, then announced the schedule to the members via the monthly newsletter.

"I just want to make sure you have a decent schedule of rides," Bristol snipped, offending Kara.

Kara did not inform Bristol of the next trail committee meeting. They presented their schedule at the next board meeting. Bristol handed out a schedule of her own to the board members. "I think you'll like mine better. It has a good mix of local and out-of-the area rides. It has one weekend ride each month, and two day rides each month." She gave Kara a haughty look as she passed out her own papers.

Kara felt blindsided. When the group had time to read, Bristol ordered, "I want a show of hands accepting my ride schedule."

"Just wait a minute, Bristol," Luke Musser stopped her. "How about the trail committee's *official* proposal? And how about a discussion? I, for one, think they have a great schedule with a good mix of rides."

There was a murmur of agreement.

Kara smiled at Luke's use of the word "official."

Without being called on, someone moved to accept the official proposal of the trail committee and another member seconded the motion.

Bristol fumed. "You can't do that! It wasn't called for by the president."

"It's already in the minutes," the secretary spoke up. "Go ahead and call for the vote."

Just as Bristol was about to hit her gavel, the board members began raising their hands saying, "I accept."

Luke confirmed, "The trail committee's schedule was voted on and passed. Thank you, Kara, to you and your committee for a job well done."

Bristol felt her control of the meeting running away, but she did not know how to bring it back. After that night, she gave both Luke and Kara her cold shoulder. She made snide remarks to others about Kara until Kara finally quit the club. She told her friends she would be back if Bristol ever left.

During their club Christmas party, Paulette Parsons sat down on what seemed to be an available seat. Bristol came back in the room and stood leaning over her to demand her seat back, in a loud voice, nearly yelling, hands on hips.

"Why would you take my seat? All these other seats are available. Why would you take mine?"

Paulette, embarrassed, murmured, "I'm sorry. I didn't know it was yours, Bristol."

"Well, you saw my purse on the floor! You should have known it was my seat."

"No, I didn't notice it. Here, sit down. I'll move over by Becky. I'd be happy to sit by her."

Paulette stood up to move and Bristol barked, "Never mind now. You stole my seat and I don't want it now. I'll sit at the head of the table where I belong." She stalked off.

Paulette moved to the empty seat next to Becky who tried to smooth over the situation. "Don't worry about her. Most people know how venal she is." They chatted a few minutes when Becky suggested they use the restroom. "The dinner's gonna' be served in a few minutes and I have to go."

Both women were in stalls when Bristol came in with Carla, a new member.

Carla asked Bristol, "What were you yelling at Paulette for? What was that all about?"

Not bothering to check whether anyone else was in the restroom, or just not caring, Bristol answered, "Oh, she took my seat. I even had my purse there. When I told her it was my seat, she became very rude and refused to move. She's always so nasty and selfish."

Finished, Paulette left her stall and confronted Bristol. "Bristol, you know that's not true. As soon as you told me it was your seat, I told you I was sorry, and that I wouldn't mind sitting next to Becky. Please keep it straight."

"Now you're calling me a liar! See, Carla, I told you she's a nasty one."

Just then Becky came out of her stall and lit into Bristol. "No, Bristol. Paulette never name called you. She only spoke the truth about what happened. Anyway, your purse was on the floor mostly under the table. Neither of us saw it there. Plus, she was never rude, and she gave the seat up immediately." Becky turned her back on Bristol to wash her hands.

Bristol was not going to give up. "See, Carla, Becky is Paulette's friend. She's just going to stick up for her right or wrong."

There was no winning an argument with Bristol. Becky and Paulette were finished. As they left the restroom, Paulette turned to Carla. "You'll see."

"She already saw what you're like," Bristol announced to the closing door.

Carla did see there was conflict in the club she had recently joined. She decided not to use her membership. She never attended another club function. Paulette was worried Bristol was ruining her reputation with her lies and was too embarrassed to return. Becky hung in there until she found out Bristol was waging a telephone campaign against her, gossiping and lying.

Other members quit, either because of the constant conflict Bristol created, or because of direct assaults from Bristol. One of the board members, Luke, called a special meeting and asked them to keep it secret from Bristol. At the meeting, they discussed Bristol's negative effect on the club membership. They voted to ask her to leave the club.

...

Through the years, Bristol made a few friends then dropped them when she discovered a new friend she liked better. Others dropped her when they discovered her venality.

She was not close with her daughter whom she saw

infrequently when Sophia dropped by to visit Ric. Bristol was upset when Sophia announced she was pregnant, soon to make Bristol a grandmother.

"Don't expect me to babysit," was her response to the announcement. She did not give Sophia a baby shower.

Ric made attempts to please Bristol, but nothing seemed to work. He ended up working longer hours at his job, mainly to stay away from home and her scathing remarks. When he was home, he spent as much time outdoors as he could.

Riding her horse was Bristol's only real happiness whether alone or with a current friend.

Bristol was sixty-five, friendless, and lonely when she met Nancy.

4 NANCY

Everyone was surprised. Mary Stouffer, the mother, was shocked. The daughters, Nancy and Abigail, were incredulous. The father, Donald Stouffer, was rather stunned himself, even though he was the one who did it.

Mary had wanted her daughters to learn to play the piano. Without a piano in their home, they would not be able to practice, and lessons would not be worthwhile. Don worked in construction making a decent living for his family, but he was laid-off most of the winter months. They had enough, but not much extra.

Mary had a plan. For the last seven years, she had been placing the savings from her weekly grocery allowance into a coffee can in the back of the cupboard. Sometimes she had done without a new dress, a new blouse, or a new pair of shoes longer than she preferred. She placed the value of what she did without into the coffee can which slowly began to fill up. Now and then she would take a wad of ones, fives, and tens to the bank to exchange for a fifty-dollar bill to save space in her can.

Abigail, or Sis, as the family called her, was fourteen, almost fifteen. Nancy had just turned thirteen. The family had just returned from church. Mary had a roast beef with potatoes, carrots, and onions in the oven for their Sunday dinner. It would not be ready for another half hour. The aroma of the cooking meal was mouthwatering.

Mary sent her girls to set the table while she sat down to enjoy reading the Sunday paper. It was only a few minutes later that Mary let out a whoop and hurried to the kitchen. Climbing on a small stool, she reached into the back of the cupboard for her hoard. Still on the stool, she opened the coffee can, counted her money stash, and fist-pumped the air with an exclaimed, "Yes!"

Puzzled, the sisters came into the kitchen to see what was going on with their mother. They were surprised to see her standing on the kitchen stool holding a wad of cash and laughing.

"Mom, where did that come from? Did you just find it in the cupboard?" Nancy asked.

"How did you know to look there and find it? How did you live here all this time and never see it before?" Abigail questioned.

"Silly girls, I put it here myself, and now there's enough," Mary answered as she stepped from the stool and recounted the money to be sure.

"Enough for what?" Both girls wanted to know.

"Yeah, what? That's a lot!"

"Go call your father. "I'll tell you together." Mary was grinning.

Nancy left to call her father to the kitchen. Abigail gently took the money from her mother's hand and counted it. "My goodness, Mom, how did you get all this?"

"Mary, what is that?" Don asked, as he and Nancy came into the kitchen.

"Well, it's money, Don, enough money for a piano. Now, all of you go on into the dining room and sit down. I'll bring in the roast beef and explain it to you as we eat."

Reluctantly, Mary's family had to wait until the food was on the table and grace said.

"How many times have I told you girls I want you to learn to play the piano? I've been saving this money for the last seven years. I know it isn't enough for a brand-new piano, but I was hoping to find a good used one. Today in the classified ads there's one for a more than reasonable price based on the ads I've been seeing. Don, as soon as dinner is over, I want you to take this money and the truck, and go pick up that piano. These girls are going to have piano lessons! Piano is the best basis for learning music theory, and a great background for learning to play any other instrument." Mary grinned and looked at the others in turn.

"Well?" she asked them.

"OK, I'll go pick up the piano today. Pass the food," an astonished Don agreed.

Three hours later, Don pulled into their drive with an empty bed in the pickup. It was followed by another truck pulling a small two-horse trailer.

"Look, girls, the piano is here," Mary told them as she headed for the door. The three went outside to watch the unloading of the piano. Don had parked and was approaching the man who was walking to the back of his trailer. Mary was happy Don was going to have help bringing the piano into the house.

The man opened the back of the trailer, disappeared inside, and just as the gals expected to see their new piano, a horse backed out of the trailer.

"What did you do!" Mary cried out in shock.

Nancy was speechless.

Abigail, although incredulous that it happened, understood. "Dad, you went to buy a piano and came back with a horse!" She began laughing.

"Meet Top Notch," Don said sheepishly as he stroked the silky neck.

...

The Stouffer family lived on a four-acre parcel of land in Portage County. Don and Mary bought the place to raise their family in a wholesome, rural setting. Don had always wanted to grow a large garden, and Mary was willing to can and freeze the produce to serve her family healthy, organic food.

The house was an attractive, although not fancy, three bedroom. It needed some updating, which Don did himself during the winter months while he was laid-off from his construction job. It had a small, two horse barn in back. Don used one of the stalls to store his gardening equipment.

On the day of the horse fiasco, Don set up the second stall to house the horse which came with three bales of hay, a bag of grain, a water bucket, and a bag of sawdust for bedding. "Enough to get us started into horse ownership," he told his girls as they watched him in wonderment. "You can borrow some books on horse care from the library. I'll show you what the man showed me when I bought him. Don't say anything to Mom, but there's enough money left to buy a saddle and bridle so you can ride him. Next weekend we'll go to this tack shop the guy told me about to pick up whatever else we'll need. He said sometimes they sell used saddles there."

At the time, they had accepted the fact that their mother would be arranging piano lessons for them without caring either way. The horse, however, thrilled them.

"Dad, I don't know what happened, but I'm glad you brought us a horse instead of a piano," Nancy told him.

"Me too," Abigail agreed as she stroked Top Notch's soft nose. "I just hope Mom is OK about it. Do you think she'll make you take it back?"

"Not when I explain about the disrepair the piano was in and how the guy was already loading the horse into the trailer to take him to an auction. He said maybe I'd be interested in buying the horse since I didn't want the piano. He said the horse would probably be sold to a meat buyer for dog food. That took me up short, and I started looking closely at the horse. He's only eight years old. The kids there rode him in 4H horse shows. I thought you girls would spend more time with a horse than with a piano, and it didn't seem right to send this beautiful guy to be slaughtered."

"Oh, poor Top Notch. They didn't love you anymore," Abigail cried into his mane.

"Don't worry, Top Notch. You aren't a poor fellow, you're a lucky fellow. Lucky Dad got there in time to save you. We'll take good care of you," Nancy told him. "Hey, I know some kids from school who are in a 4H club. We can join, too, and learn about horses, and have some fun showing."

Don was right about Mary accepting the horse. She only gave him a cold shoulder for two uncomfortable days. When she heard how Top Notch was headed for the meat buyers, and she saw how happy her girls were to have a horse, she gave in, and all was forgiven. "But you three will have all the care of that animal. I don't want to have to go traipsing out back to the barn to deal with it," she declared.

Mary became more involved with the horse than she anticipated, although it was indirectly. She drove her daughters to and from 4H meetings. She listened to the girls as they talked about their club meetings and events. She enthusiastically cheered them on at the Friday night horse shows. She made cookies at home for their club to sell at the shows and worked concession stand shifts.

The various Portage County 4H clubs came together at the fairgrounds each Friday night to compete with their horses and ponies. It was always a huge family affair, fast paced, tense, full of hustle and bustle. Everywhere were horses with riders, horses being led, horses being groomed, horses being tacked, and horses waiting their turn at the gate to enter their class. There were chestnuts, sorrels, palominos, blacks, pintos, and a leopard appaloosa. A second ring next to the show ring was sometimes used for warming up horses. Other times, classes were held there simultaneously, adding to the frantic hustle to make the classes on time. "I just finished Showmanship in Ring A and they called for my Walk/Trot Cloverleaf Barrels class in Ring B, gotta run!" Numerous family groups were gathered together helping the children prepare for the ring, trying to sit the kids down long enough to eat, find missing tack, watch their kids' performances in the ring. The announcer called for the next class to be ready, called the times on the contest events, called for the four-wheeler to enter the ring to drag the dirt smooth again. The small building with the food concession was crowded with people jostling to buy sloppy Joes and hot dogs, and with people signing up for classes.

In just one Friday night, a horse used its tongue to unlatch its stall door and cavort through the crowd of people, horses, and dogs, until he was caught and tied inside the stall. A horse running the barrels bucked his rider off and ran circles in the ring bucking and farting. It took fifteen people holding hands and stretching their line across the ring to slowly approach the miscreant horse and gradually slow him down and corner him. The young rider was not hurt. When the night was over, one kid was left at the fairground by a family that had used two vehicles and each parent thought the boy was in the other's truck. After reaching home, the father had to go back to pick him up.

The show season culminated in Fair Week at the end of August.

...

The Stouffer family enjoyed the years of 4H together. In March of Abigail's senior high school year, she announced she was ready to discontinue riding. "I want to take a summer school class in chemistry before going to nursing school in the fall. I'm not going to have time for 4H anymore."

"Well!" her mother responded. The family was gathered around the Sunday dinner table after church. "What about you, Nancy? Are you staying in 4H?"

"Actually, I've been thinking about trail riding more like our 4H club did a couple of times. I liked that better than competitive classes in a ring with all the stress. I mean, 4H has been fun, but I loved the serenity and beauty of the forest trails. We already have our horse trailer with living quarters, but I would love a smooth gaited horse like a Tennessee Walker for spending hours comfortably on trail. What do you think, Dad? Could we go horse camping?"

"I'll have to think it over. Umm, let's see. Well, I don't see why not, do you, Mary?"

Mary shook her head no and shrugged her shoulders.

"But what about Top Notch? You don't want to trail ride him?"

"I'd rather find a smooth gaited horse, but I could ride him until I do."

Some searching on-line resulted in finding a horse auction for quality horses to be held near Clarion, Pennsylvania, in May, at Ray Smith's Cook Forest Scenic Trail Rides. There would be no meat buyers there, only those looking for decent ranch horses and trail horses. After much discussion, the Stouffers decided it would be a safe place to sell Top Notch, and there would be a good possibility for Nancy to find her smooth gaited, experienced, trail horse.

The weekend of the horse auction approached. Don and Mary were concerned the early May weather would be too cold, especially in the higher elevation in Pennsylvania. Their horse trailer had living quarters, but the furnace had quit working last fall and they had stored the trailer over the winter without having fixed it. Nancy and Abigail assured their parents they remained enthusiastic about going. Abigail was definitely finished with horses and all of the chores that came with them. Top Notch was for sale, and no, she would not be sorry to see him go. Nancy wanted to own a smooth gaited horse and spend hours trail riding. The auction was a good chance to find a healthy one at a decent price. If Top Notch sold, his price would be put toward the purchase of the new one.

"Ok, girls," Don told them. "If you can hack the cold, wet weather, I'll drive you up there. Your mother's going to stay home."

"Yes, I'll stay here, but I'm going to make you some soup to take so you'll have something nutritious and hot to keep you warm. I'll put all the spare blankets in the camper for you, too. Take long johns and your winter coats, hats and gloves," Mary advised.

"Mom, it's not going to be all that cold," Nancy told her. "It's May, for goodness sake."

...

They were headed to Ray's annual spring horse auction. After driving for three hours Friday, Don pulled the rig into Ray's horse camp just before dark. After selecting their camp site, Don backed the rig into place. Together they chose two trees to suspend the chain that would be the picket line for Top Notch.

Don pointed to two trees he thought would work.

"No!" the sisters chorused together.

"They're too close. Top Notch will eat the bark and that would kill the trees," Nancy explained.

"Yeah, that wouldn't be good," Abigail added. "How about these two?" She pointed.

This time Don disagreed. "No, too close to the front of the truck. He could kick it, and he'd be on the other side of the tack room door, not as convenient for feeding and clean up. How about those two?"

This time everyone agreed.

It turned out to be colder than the girls had anticipated, only in the low forties. They set up camp wearing their winter clothing. Abigail grabbed the mounting block from the trailer and placed it near one of the chosen trees. Nancy pulled out a hay bag made of rope and stuffed an entire bale of hay into it. The horse would be able to pull tufts of hay through the open sections between the rope netting as it hung on the picket line. Setting the filled hay bag aside, she filled a bucket with water for the horse.

Don used the mounting block to gain the height he wanted to wrap the chain around the first tree. The end of the chain that circled the tree had been slipped through a piece of fire hose to protect the bark. Don jumped down, and Abigail moved the mounting block down. Don stretched the chain across, stepped up, and wrapped this end of chain around the second tree, again using firehose for protection. Abigail handed him the come-a-long, and Don ratcheted the chain tight.

Abigail moved the mounting block to the center of the picket line and stepped up. Nancy handed up the bag of hay. As Nancy pushed up from the bottom, Abigail used double end brass snaps to hook the hay to the chain. She attached one end of each snap through the rope of the hay bag, and the other end into a loop of chain until the bag hung close to the chain.

"That looks good, Sis. I don't think it will come down too low," Nancy told her. As the horse ate the hay, the bag would tend to sink lower, and the horse could tangle in the rope bag.

With the picket line up and the hay bale hung, Abigail opened the rear of the horse trailer for Top Notch. She untied him and backed him out. After attaching him to the picket line with his lead rope, she offered him water from the bucket. Top Notch dipped his nose into the bucket and drank deeply, then began working on the hay, pulling wisps through the rope bag and chewing contentedly.

Don leveled the trailer. Abigail refilled the water bucket and placed it under one of the trees at the end of the picket line, handy, but not where Top Notch could knock it over. She put a serving of grain in a bucket and hung it for the horse. Nancy cleaned out the manure from the stall in the back of the trailer, shoveling it into a large, plastic bucket that fit onto a folding trolley. Abigail scouted the area for a place to dump the manure and found a three-sided wooden frame where others had dumped. It was large enough for a front-end loader to dig it out for disposal in a more permanent site.

It was now dark enough to need their flashlights.

"Well, girls, what do you think? Are we done yet?" Don rubbed his hands together for warmth.

"Yeah, I'm done, how about you, Sis?" Nancy zipped up her jacket. She had warmed herself up while shoveling the manure and had unzipped it.

Abigail answered, "Well, I have to dump this manure, then take down the grain bucket and offer Top some more water. Then I'm done. How about you heat up some water to make us hot chocolate?"

"That sounds good, girls. It'll warm us up."

Don and Nancy went into the living quarters of the horse trailer. Nancy had the hot chocolate ready by the time Abigail joined them.

"Your mother put six blankets on my bed." Don would be sleeping on the sofa bed. "You gals have four blankets, but you should be warm enough sleeping double up there in the gooseneck." He blew on his cocoa to cool it before taking a sip.

"Sis, are you sure you're ready to let Top Notch go?"

"Yes, Daddy. I don't have the time for him anymore, so it's not fair to keep him. I'll be in nursing school this fall, remember. He needs to find another home where he'll have more attention and love."

"Nancy?"

"Yeah, he belongs in another 4H home, or where he can teach some other kids to ride. I'm ready for a Tennessee Walker or Missouri Fox Trotter and long trail rides."

"OK, girls, but if you change your minds, we can haul him back home. It's not too late until the auctioneer starts the bidding on him."

They took their turns getting ready for bed in the small bathroom. Don turned the sofa into his bed and the girls climbed up to the double bed in the gooseneck, the higher part of the trailer above the bed of the truck. The many blankets kept them warm in the cold.

Nancy had a tough time falling asleep. Her mind kept thinking about the auction the next day. She wondered if she would find her horse here. She was excited. Her sister went to sleep beside her almost instantly. Nancy said silent prayers of thanksgiving for her loving family and asked that all the horses sold tomorrow would find good homes. At last, cozy under the covers while the temperature dropped outside, she fell asleep.

…

The next morning, they awoke with temperatures in the mid-thirties. Large, soft flakes of snow were falling, but melting when they hit the ground. Abigail went outside to give Top Notch grain and water, and to clean up the manure under the picket line. Don helped her to put up a fresh bale of hay. Nancy made them a hot breakfast of bacon, eggs, and camp toast. They were not plugged into electricity, so Nancy toasted the buttered bread on both sides in an iron skillet on their propane stove.

After breakfast clean up, they strolled around the horse camp. At the far end was a large covered arena with huge double doors open at both ends. Inside were maybe four hundred folding chairs set up around tables loaded with the horse tack to be auctioned starting at ten o'clock. The tack would be sold first. Everything imaginable horse related was piled on the tables and the sand floor around them. There were saddles, bridles, halters, lead lines, brass snaps, manure forks, manure buckets, water buckets, grazing muzzles, brushes, curry combs, leather ties, cinches, vet wrap, saddle racks, trailer ties, curb chains, hoof polish, mane and tail conditioners, buggy whips, training whips, electrolyte powders, bags of horse treats, and on and on.

The horses were scheduled to be auctioned starting around two o'clock in the afternoon. Looking around at the number of items, Nancy thought the tack auction would not finish by two. The auctioneer would have to move them plenty fast.

Four people sat at a long table inside the door to register bidders. A long line was already forming to register.

"Girls, do you see anything here you need?" Don asked his daughters.

"No, Daddy, I don't. I'm kind of getting out of horses, you know," Abigail told him. She wandered outside to find out how to enter Top Notch in the auction.

Nancy turned to Don. "I don't know. I don't think I need any tack, but maybe we register here now to bid on the horses. Let's get in line." She took his hand to lead him through the growing crowd to the back of the line.

People were congregated in small groups, chatting. Nancy and Don stepped into what they thought was the end of the line and were told the end was farther down. Don apologized and they moved past, asking each small group conversing if they were in line. Each time, they were. They finally found the end of the line, all the way outside.

They saw Abigail in another, shorter, line outside. Nancy waved.

"I'll go find out what's going on with her. You stay in line here," Don instructed.

"Daddy, this is where I have to register Top Notch for the auction," Abigail explained. "I think I have to pay an auction fee. Do you have the checkbook with you?"

"Yes, Honey, I'll take care of it. I'll wait in line with you, then we'll catch up with Nancy."

The sky was gray even though it was mid-morning. The soft snow flakes were becoming wetter, more like sleet. Nancy's place in line was finally under the roof of the arena, but it was still moving slowly. Don explained that he would join her after helping her sister register the horse.

Outside, two people sat at a table under a canopy registering horses that would be auctioned. Abigail had moved up to third in line. As they stood there in the sleety snow, young men and women were riding horses back and forth in front of the arena, showing them off. Some of them galloped past, despite the crowd. Sometimes they brought them to a roll-back stop, where the horse would abruptly lean back on its haunches from a gallop and slide to a stop. Sometimes they would spin the horse. It was impressive and gained the attention of potential buyers.

When it was Abigail's turn, she told the women behind the table she wanted to sell her horse.

"Well, this is the place for that. If you want to bid, you have to go to the other line."

"No, yes, I'm selling my horse." Her eyes were drawn to a young man who was now standing up on his saddle to prove how steady and reliable his horse was.

"Did you preregister? Is your horse in the catalog?" The woman drew her back to the business at hand.

"No, I didn't know about that. I thought you just brought the horse here this morning." Abigail looked worried.

"That's all right. You can do it this way. There's a fifty-dollar auction fee to put him in the ring, then, if he sells, eight percent of the sale price is taken out of your check. You pay the fifty dollars now. Can you do that?"

"Yes, we can do that." She turned to her father who was stepping to the table to write the check.

"Do you want someone to ride your horse for you? You pay them twenty dollars and they'll ride it around out here to show it off and even ride it in the auction ring for you." The woman took Don's check.

"I don't need that. I'll ride my own horse."

"Here's number thirty-nine. It's a good number. You don't want to be near the first or the last. There'll be almost a hundred horses auctioned today. Put this sticker on your horse's rump." The woman handed the sticker to Abigail.

Ready to write, she asked her the horse's name, breed, and gender, and whether she had registration papers and health certificate for him.

"His name is Top Notch. He's kind of a quarter horse cross, I guess, no papers. I do have his health certificate."

"You hand the papers to the guy in the ring. He'll give them to the auctioneer. They'll go with the horse, if he sells. Do you have a minimum selling price? If he doesn't go for that, you don't have to sell him."

"I don't know. I'll have to think about that."

Forgetting to ask about the logistics, Abigail thanked her and turned away. It was Don who asked where to take the horse and how to know when it was time to bring him into the arena to be sold.

"The horse auction will be right inside the arena here after the tack auction. They'll take down all the tables from the tack sale and set up a ring. You can ride your horse inside the ring when it's your turn. You are going to ride, aren't you? They sell better if you ride them instead of leading them."

Abigail and Don both nodded yes.

The woman went on. "Just pay attention to the numbers as they enter the arena. They go pretty much in order. If you're there when it's your number, you go in. If you're not there, they go to the next one and take you when you get there. You enter from the other end of the building. Do you want to say anything about your horse? Tell the people about him so they want to bid?"

"I guess so. How do I do that?"

"Just tell the guy in the pen you want to talk about your horse, and he'll hand you the mic. Don't worry. You'll do fine."

The woman reached out her hand to the next person in line, and Abigail and Don left to catch up with Nancy. They had to squeeze past a crowd of people to join her in line. The chairs were all taken, and people were standing four and five deep in the wide doorway of the arena. They finally crammed their way through to her.

"Top Notch is registered for the sale," Abigail reported.

"Man, this line is slow," Nancy complained. "It's kind of cold, too. I can't believe so many people turned out. What's it doing outside?"

"The sleet is turning into a light rain, so it must be getting a little warmer," Abigail informed her. "But when you're done here, you should go outside to watch the horses being ridden. It's really cool to see the riders showing them off."

"Yeah, maybe I can see someone riding a gaited horse so I can check it out. I wonder if you can ride them yourself before buying?" Nancy was eager to find her dream horse. She would be even more keyed up if not for the cold and damp.

"Don't let anyone ride Top Notch," Don warned Abigail. "We don't want the liability. Anyway, it should be enough for a potential buyer to see a slight young girl like you handle him with ease."

"OK, Daddy. I won't. Hey, do you guys smell food? It smells like sloppy Joes to me! Yum!" Abigail rubbed her tummy.

"You hungry already?" Actually, Don was, too.

"Yeah, I am. It must be the cold. The food tent's just outside. I'm going to see what they're selling."

"OK, Sis." Don gave his permission. "Maybe we can get a hot sandwich to go with Mom's soup back in the trailer."

When Abigail reported back, Don told her to put their mother's soup on the stove to warm, then come back to stand in the food line. "When we're done here, we'll find you in that line. A burger sounds good to me."

When Nancy had her bidding number, she and her father joined Abigail in the food line just in time to order. They each covered their hot sandwich with a napkin in an attempt to keep it dry and hurried back to the trailer where the soup was hot. It felt good to be in the trailer out of the wet drizzle and the chill breeze. It was surprising how much the trailer had warmed with day light and the heat of the stove.

Suddenly there was a loud crack, then another, and another.

"What was that?" the sisters exclaimed in unison.

"I don't know, but I don't think it was gun shots," their father answered. "It seems that the rain has let up. Let's finish up here then get Top ready to ride. Sis, you need to warm him up and get him used to the crowd before you take him into the arena."

As they groomed Top Notch and saddled him, they heard the explosive cracks again. Crack! Crack! Crack! As the girls worked to saddle the horse, Don walked back to the arena area. He returned with an explanation.

"One of those kids riding the horses has a bullwhip. He stands up on the saddle and cracks the whip to show the steadiness of the horse. Never saw anything like it. Guess the horse is steady! It's something."

Abigail untied Top Notch from the picket line.

"Do you want the mounting block or a leg up?" her father asked her.

"No, I'll just jump up." Abigail used the reins to turn her horse's head slightly toward her as she stood on his left side. She put her left foot in the stirrup and easily swung onto the saddle. The horse stood quietly while she adjusted the stirrups. "Don't worry, I'll ride around here for awhile before going down to the arena. He'll be OK." Abigail moved her horse forward.

Don stood watching the pair for a minute then caught up to Nancy, who had started back to the arena.

"Look how many cars, trucks, and horse trailers are here now, Daddy." Nancy waved her hand to include them all. "I hope it doesn't mean the horse I want to buy will be bid too high."

"Remember, you don't have to buy a horse today. You want the *right* horse, not just *a* horse."

They dodged trucks, trailers, horses, and people. In front of the arena, the riders were still showing off horses. The tack auction continued. The auctioneer could be heard outside.

"Look," Don pointed out. "There's that kid with the bullwhip."

The young man in blue jeans, western shirt and boots, no jacket, was standing on the saddle again, this time with a long, blue tarp wrapped across the horse's neck. He cracked the bull whip on one side of the horse, then on the other side. The whip dropped to the ground as he bent to pick up the tarp. Lifting the tarp, he stood back up and shook the tarp over the horse's neck and face.

"I don't know, Daddy. It's impressive in a way, but stupid, too. Look at the tight muscles in that horse's neck."

The guy slipped from a standing position on the saddle to sit on it again. He leaned far over to his right to reach for the bull whip on the ground. That's when the horse exploded. With the first buck, the rider came off, twisting backward to land on his feet. By then, the horse had bucked its way forward toward a green jeep parked just in front of the food tent. The rider was clear of the bucking horse, but people were scrambling to move out of the way of its kicking back feet and its forward momentum. People eating under the food tent left their lunches to scramble clear.

Don shielded Nancy, who thought that the horse was going to land in the back of the jeep. She was worried it was going to injure itself on the jeep or in the guywires of the tent. At the last moment, the horse stood still, its sides heaving with the effort. The embarrassed rider caught up the reins and jumped back onto the saddle.

The horse auction did not start until after three o'clock. Nancy spent her time running back and forth from the arena to where her sister was riding Top Notch. She kept her informed of the number of the horse being auctioned at the moment so Abigail would have an idea when it would be her turn. All the while, Nancy was on the lookout for a gaited horse. However, the horses all seemed to be quarter horse type ranch horses.

When horse twenty-nine entered the pen, Nancy told her sister to ride to the arena. "I went behind the arena to see where you go. There's a paddock area in front of the doors where a bunch of riders are waiting their turn. You should wait there to get Top used to the noise of the auction. Every time someone makes a bid, some guy blows a whistle really loud. I hope it won't scare Top and make him look spooky."

Abigail turned her horse toward the arena. It was then Nancy heard the distinct sound of a four-beat hoof pattern and she turned to see a beautiful black horse with white blaze seeming to glide down the camp road. The rider seemed to float along with the horse. There was no up and down motion, only forward movement. The beauty of it took Nancy's breath.

She cut through some camp sites to intercept the horse and rider. "Hey! Excuse me!"

The rider pulled up and looked down at Nancy, who asked him, "Is this horse in the auction? Is it a Tennessee Walker?"

"It certainly is a Walker. She's number fifty-two. You buying today?"

"Maybe. Tell me about your horse."

The man told her the horse was a four-year-old mare with breed registration papers and a health certificate. It was up-to-date on its preventative shots and had just been seen by the equine dentist who floated, or filed, its teeth. The farrier had put new shoes on the front, and it was bare foot in the back.

"You can see she's a good-going horse. She's dropped a colt that's coming two years old. I'm keeping him and selling her.

You'd be getting a good horse and you could breed her for another one. I've ridden her on trails all over."

Nancy was wistful. "Trail riding is what I want to do. I'm tired of just going around the ring in the 4H shows." She reached out to touch the beautiful black neck. The horse turned its head toward her.

"She's number fifty-two if you want her." With that, the man rode off, the rhythmic four-beat sound enchanting Nancy.

She ran after horse and rider, crossing camp roads to intercept their path. "Wait, wait!" she called to the rider. "Can I ride her?""

"Are you a serious buyer?"

"Yes, yes I am." Nancy pulled her bidding number from her jacket pocket to show him.

"OK, then. I'll give you a leg up." The man swung down from his tall horse and helped Nancy up. "Have you ridden a gaited horse before?"

"No, I haven't, but we have a trotting horse we rode in 4H."

"Riding these guys is a bit different to get the best gait out of them. Use both hands on the reins. Here, hold them a little tighter, just until you feel the bit, but without pulling back on it." The man adjusted the reins into Nancy's hands. "You want your weight back, but don't lean way back. You still want good posture. If she doesn't seem smooth enough at first, tighten the reins a little more while urging her on with your legs and your voice. Ready?"

Nancy nodded and the man clucked to his horse. The mare took off and was immediately into her smooth running-walk gait

Tennessee Walkers are known for. Nancy was grinning with delight. It was a much faster speed than Top Notch walked or even trotted. His trot was a three beat that had the rider rising up and down. This mare's four beat moved the pair forward with no up and down motion. It was indeed like floating, like soaring on a magic carpet.

They were flying around Ray's gravel camp roads farther from the crowded arena area. Nancy was thrilled. She knew she wanted this horse. She would have kept riding, but the horse's owner waved her back. Reluctantly, she returned the mare to him.

When she found her sister and her father, she excitedly told them about finding her dream horse. "Let's hope for a high selling price for Top Notch and a low selling price for this number fifty-two of yours," her father commented. "If that all works out, let's hope she's the horse you think she is. How about we do a little family prayer?"

The girls agreed and Don led them in a short prayer. "Father, we ask your blessings on this day for the safety of all the people and animals here. We ask that Top Notch bring a decently high price, that he goes to a good home, and if number fifty-two is the best horse for Nancy, that she brings an affordable price. We thank you for all the blessings you have given this family and for being the guide in our lives. Amen."

"Amen," the girls echoed.

...

When Abigail's turn came to enter the sale ring, she asked to talk about Top Notch. She was told to ride him around the ring two turns, then to stop for the mic. She told the crowd his age, how many 4H ribbons he had won, how he had good ground manners, and how anyone could safely ride him. She handed back the mic and continued to ride her horse around the ring while the auctioneer called for bids.

The crowd was reluctant to begin bidding, and the auctioneer had to lower his suggested, opening bid three times. Nancy and Don groaned as they watched Sis ride around and around the ring. Finally, someone in the crowd agreed to the auctioneer's call for a bid of five hundred dollars. That was a lesser amount than what Top Notch would go for meat price. That was unacceptable to everyone in the family. They would call it a no-sale.

Abigail urged her horse into as fast of a canter as he could manage in the small ring and quickly pulled him to an abrupt stop. It was not a roll back stop, but it demonstrated how responsive the horse was. Then she cut across the center of the ring in the slow canter, changing leads every third step. The crowd clapped and bid higher.

Abigail stopped center ring. She dropped her reins to the ground, put pressure in her stirrups to stand in the saddle, then eased her feet from the stirrups as she leaned over the saddle horn.

"No, Sis, no! Don't do it, don't do it," Nancy murmured.

"What is she doing?" Don asked, but he immediately found out as Abigail placed her feet on the saddle behind her and unsteadily stood up. She carefully waved her arms over her head before quickly sitting back down. The crowd clapped and bid higher.

"Have you two been practicing that crazy stunt?" her father asked Nancy.

"No, I would bet that's the first time Sis ever tried it. I think she has enough trust in Top she was willing to risk it to up his price. Look, it's working."

Higher bids were coming quicker.

Abigail rode Top Notch to the rail and stopped nose to rail, rump toward center ring. She then asked him to back, which he did without hesitation and as straight as a two by four. Abigail stopped him just before his rump hit the rail on the other side of the ring.

The bidding slowed as only two competing bidders were left. The auctioneer no longer called for fifty dollar increases at a time. Neither bidder was willing to give another fifty. He asked for another twenty-five dollars and received a "no" headshake in answer. He asked for another ten dollars. No. Another five dollars. No.

"Going once for twenty-five-fifty. The auctioneer hesitated momentarily, then, "Going twice." He waited a second. "Sold for two thousand five hundred fifty dollars. Next horse."

Abigail rode from the ring where a scolding from her father waited for trying the foolish stunt of standing on her horse. However, they were all three pleased with the sale price. Even though many horses brought more, there were also horses that sold for much less. Nancy hoped that number fifty-two would go for much less.

Waiting was hard for Nancy. She kept watching for the black mare, but she did not see her again until number forty-five was called into the sale ring. The man rode his horse back and forth in front of the arena, listening for each number to be called next. Nancy watched them float up and down the road until number fifty was called. The man then turned the horse toward the back of the arena to wait his turn to enter the ring. Nancy found her father, and they entered the arena to be ready for the bidding. There were seats for them because so many people had bought or sold what they wanted and left.

"Good luck, Nancy," Abigail told her as they sat down.

“Thanks, Sis. I’m nervous about this.”

“Come on now, relax,” their father advised. “We prayed for this to happen if it’s for the best. If it doesn’t happen, we will feel there is something better in store for you.”

“Yeah, I know, and I believe it, but I can’t help feeling I want this horse to be the best for me and for it to work out to be mine. Wait ‘til you ride her!”

Nancy grabbed her sister’s arm as horse number fifty-one was sold and left the arena. Fifty-two was entering!

“She really is pretty,” Abigail told Nancy.

Don held their bidding number and waited to make his first bid. He had been studying the bidding and had a strategy in mind. The auctioneer began with a price that was higher than the crowd wanted. Finally, someone made an opening bid when the auctioneer lowered the price sufficiently. Don held back as the auctioneer asked for the next bid. He wanted to test the interest in the crowd for this horse. It looked like there were only three people bidding. When they slowed down, and the auctioneer asked for the next fifty-dollar increment, Don raised his number and nodded. The auctioneer’s helper yelled, “Here!” blew his whistle, and pointed at Don.

Don was hoping his late bid would encourage the other three remaining bidders to drop out. One did, but one of the other two nodded yes to the next fifty-dollar increment. The auctioneer asked for the next fifty-dollar increment and Don shouted “Yes!” enthusiastically. He hoped his enthusiasm would cause the last two bidders to feel that Don would pay any amount for the horse and make them give up before the price rose too far.

The auctioneer called for the next fifty-dollar increment and Don shouted, “Yes!” while rising to his feet waving his number. The girls giggled at their normally mild-mannered father.

Don turned red as the auctioneer told him the top bid was already his and asked the other two bidders if they would go up fifty. One shook his head no and left the arena. The other one shook his head no, and the auctioneer asked him for a twenty-five-dollar increase. The man nodded yes, but Don realized the man was nearly done and agreed to another twenty-five-dollar increase.

"I have eighteen-fifty, eighteen-fifty, how about eighteen-seventy-five. Eighteen-seventy-five, eighteen-seventy-five. Give me just eighteen-seventy-five. How about eighteen-seventy-five?" The auctioneer was looking at the last man competing with Don. He nodded no and the auctioneer tried for eighteen-seventy, then eighteen-sixty-five, then eighteen-sixty, but the man was done.

"Eighteen-fifty once, eighteen-fifty twice, sold for eighteen hundred fifty dollars. Next horse."

Nancy jumped up and let out a wild hoop that had the crowd laughing. She ran out of the arena to find her new horse. Don went to the check-out table to pay.

Nancy had her first easy-gaited horse, a Tennessee Walker. She called her Lola because it was the barn name she came with. The name on her registration papers was much longer.

...

Nancy spent many hours riding Lola on day rides at local bridle trails and farther from home on weekend camp outs. Before she turned eighteen, her father drove the truck and trailer. The spring Nancy graduated from high school, Don taught her how to drive the rig. He still went with her each time for the next several years. Mary often joined them on the camping trips, taking along her knitting and a good book.

Although she and her family joined the Portage County chapter of the Ohio Horseman's Council, and they attended club functions including group rides, Nancy did not meet anyone of interest to date. She met no one eligible at her job as an aide in an assisted living home. Once, when Abigail jokingly told Nancy she should check out an online dating site, Nancy thought her sister was serious. She had always hoped to meet her mate in church, but there were no eligible bachelors attending her family's church. After reading several reviews of an online Christian dating site, she signed up. By then she was twenty-nine years old and concerned about becoming an old maid.

She did not tell her parents at first, only her sister, who was home for a weekend visit from her nursing position in a Dayton hospital four hours away from the family home. They were in Nancy's bedroom with the door shut.

"He seems so nice. He says, well, types, all the right things. His name is Harry Reynolds. He said he lives in Kent. I only told him my first name and that I live in Portage County, too. He doesn't mind that I still live with my parents. He said he goes to church! I wish I could sneak in some Sunday and observe him without anyone noticing, but I'm afraid to try."

"Oh, Nancy, I worry about you going online to date. You don't know anyone who knows this guy and can vouch for him." Abigail stretched out on Nancy's bed and put her hands behind her head. "I wish you could find someone on your own."

"Why don't you introduce me to one of your hunky doctors? Of course, the dear doctor would have to be interested in horses." Nancy picked up her hairbrush and ran it through her hair, then leaned back on her dresser.

"Doctors are too busy to be interested in horses. Anyway, I doubt you would want to move so far away. You might as well meet someone around here. Tell me more about this Reynolds guy."

Eventually Abigail agreed Harry sounded like he would be worth meeting. "But you'll have to tell Mom and Dad. And set something up so you'll be safe. It would be ideal if you two could figure out if there's at least one person you both know who could recommend him."

Nancy finally told her parents she was emailing Harry. They were not pleased, but they were supportive.

Don insisted, "We need to meet him when you do."

Mary worried, "We have to make sure you'll be safe."

Nancy let Harry know she was finally ready to meet him in person. They had moved from emails to telephone calls that sometimes lasted for two or three hours. They set up a meeting in the local Walmart store.

"I'll be sitting in the aisle where the donut display is, waiting for you," Harry told her. "See you at ten o'clock Saturday morning."

Sitting? Nancy wondered.

Abigail came up from Dayton for the big reveal. The whole family piled into the car at nine o'clock to be there early enough for a glimpse of Harry Reynolds as he walked into the Walmart.

"If he looks like a pervert, we'll just drive away with you," Don told Nancy.

"Now Don, you know there's no such look as a pervert, so maybe we should just drive away now," Mary suggested.

"Mom, look!" From the back seat, Abigail pointed to a man swaggering down the parking lot carrying a folding lawn chair. He seemed to be whistling.

Nancy slapped her sister's pointing hand down. "He certainly seems to be confident enough. I hope he isn't cocky. Yeah, I think he is whistling."

"What's he doing carrying that chair?" Mary wanted to know.

"He did tell me he would be sitting waiting for me in the donut aisle, and look how early he is. We nearly missed being early enough to see him walk in. He's kind of cute, huh?"

The family watched Harry disappear into the store.

"How long should we wait before going in?" Nancy asked.

"Wait until a few minutes after ten," her sister suggested.

"Right. Don't look too anxious," their mother agreed.

"We could go in and do some shopping around the donut aisle, check him out. Anyone want to join me?" Abigail reached for the door handle.

"Stay here!" Nancy begged. "Don't embarrass me!"

"I can't believe we're doing this," Mary uttered under her breath from the front seat.

At ten o'clock, the family decided Nancy could go in. As soon as the others watched her enter the store, they all got out of the car. They laughed when they realized they each had the same thought of following her.

Nancy hurried to the rear of the store. Two times she crept past the aisle where Harry sat on his folding lawn chair just five feet from her. The first time she peered down the aisle as she sneaked past, but he was sitting facing the front of the store with his back to her. She came back and stood looking at him, but there was nothing to see except the back of his head. She walked to the front of the store using the next aisle over. When she gathered her courage, and turned the corner ready to face Harry, there were her parents and her sister on the other side of the opening.

Instead of walking down Harry's aisle to meet him, she scurried across the opening to her family. "What are you doing here?" she hissed at them as they all stood at the end of the aisle. "Go away!"

"Shh, just go on," Abigail whispered, shooing her forward.

"I can't with all of you here. You were supposed to stay in the car and only be here to make sure I wouldn't be kidnapped."

Don sneaked a peak around the corner at the man seated on his lawn chair. Harry was grinning. Don quickly ducked back.

Mary pushed at Don. "I want to see."

Before she could look, Nancy pushed her back. "No, Mom, please just leave. All of you. Wait in the car for me like we planned."

Shoppers were passing by, giving strange looks to both the man sitting in the aisle and to the family eyeing him furtively.

"Just go," Don encouraged as he pushed Nancy forward into the aisle where Harry, at the end, saw her and grinned.

"Nancy?" he asked and stood up, or tried to, but his legs tangled in the chair that was collapsing under him. He tried to catch his balance, but he fell into the display of donuts, and the entire shelving unit fell to the floor, donut boxes smashing as he danced on top of them trying not to lose his balance and trying not to step on them but failing at both. He ended up on the floor amid the squashed boxes of donuts and grinned.

Nancy ran down the aisle to him. "Are you OK? Are you hurt?" She held out a hand to help him up.

"I'm OK. I think I just fell for you, Sweetheart. Tell your family to come on down here and meet me instead of hovering around the corner like they aren't there." Harry dusted off his blue jeans and moved his mangled chair out of the middle of the aisle. "It's really good to meet you in person, Nancy."

Introductions were made all around, and everyone pitched in to put the fallen donut boxes into an empty grocery cart. A stock boy came by, and Harry helped him lift the shelving unit back in place.

"You certainly know how to make a first impression," Don told Harry as they sat in the coffee shop next door, getting to know each other.

"Just so it's a lasting one. Just so it's a lasting one," Harry repeated looking fondly at Nancy.

It proved to be so.

Harry had swagger, but he was neither cocky nor conceited. He was confident, sure of his convictions, sure of his perceptions, sure of his decisions, and full of the joy of life. He was kind, caring, thoughtful, and loving. Nancy fell in love as she and Harry dated exclusively for the next year and a half.

Nancy was thirty-one years old when Harry showed up at her family's home leading a sleek, black horse down the drive. Mary heard Lola whinnying, and when she heard an answering cry, she went to the window. "Nancy, you better come see this," she called to her daughter.

Nancy looked out the window at the whistling man swaggering up her drive leading the beautiful, prancing horse, head and tail high, and she ran for the door.

"What are you doing?" she wanted to know. "Where did this gorgeous creature come from? What are you doing with him?"

"Well, the guy I bought him from just dropped me off in front of your drive. He went on down the road, so I hope you'll agree to my proposal." Harry dropped to one knee. "Will you marry me and let George here stay in the barn with Lola until we can buy our own place? I don't have anywhere to keep him, I don't know what to do with him, and your dad said it would be OK." Harry reached in his pocket for the ring box, opened it, and reached for Nancy's hand.

"Yes, yes, I will," she answered softly, smiling, and giving him her hand. "I've been praying for what to do about you, and I think God has just answered. So, I say yes to both of you."

The couple embraced, and Nancy's parents, who had come out to the yard, applauded.

...

Nancy and Harry were married six months later in a simple church wedding. Don and Mary sold them the home Nancy and Abigail grew up in, and moved to a home in nearby Ravenna. "Less maintenance, and still room for a small garden, and you'll have the barn for the horses," Don told them when he made the offer. Harry assured Don he would keep up the larger garden and bring produce for Mary. "I'll do my best to maintain the house the way you would, but any help from you would be appreciated," Harry told Don. "I love your daughter with all my heart, and I love her family, too. I'd do anything for any of you."

Harry and Don man-hugged awkwardly, thumping each other's backs and choking back their emotions.

Harry accompanied Nancy on day rides as often as his work schedule permitted. Nancy often worked weekends in the assisted living home. Her days off were during the week while Harry worked as a computer analyst. When they could manage weekends off together, they went camping with the horses. They both enjoyed the beauty of the forest trails. Nancy delighted in the feel of a good horse under her, but Harry enjoyed caring for the horses more than he did riding.

They eventually bought a new horse trailer to replace the old one that was wearing out. Another year they bought a new truck to haul it.

When Lola died due to old age complications, Nancy began riding George. Harry was content not to ride, so they did not buy another horse until George retired. Then came Rex. Lola, George, and Rex were Tennessee Walkers. When Rex died, they found a golden palomino Fox Trotter mare named Bright Beauty. Her walk did not have the long reach like the stride of a Walking horse, but her four-beat fox trot was smooth like the Walker's running walk gait. Beauty had good ground manners and an enormous amount of trail experience for her age.

Through the years, Nancy and Harry were happy together. However, three major events marred their nearly perfect life.

First, Nancy and Harry thought they would make excellent, loving parents who could bring up children to be responsible, independent, successful, Christian adults. They were disappointed each month when there was no pregnancy. When Nancy was finally pregnant, she had a miscarriage during her first trimester. The parents-to-be cried in each other's arms.

Second, Don died of a sudden heart attack. Harry was as devastated as Nancy, Abigail, and Mary. The family leaned on each other and their faith through the worst of their grief. Their faith that Harry was now in Heaven where they would see him again someday did not stop them from missing him on earth in the here and now.

Third, shortly after Don's passing, Mary began to have difficulty finding the words she wanted to use, and she became more forgetful than she had ever been. At first, the family blamed it on stress due to losing her husband, but as time went by, Mary's symptoms became worse. Having worked with the elderly, many who had dementia in different degrees, Nancy was the first to suspect what was happening to Mary. She talked it over with her sister who, as a nurse, was also familiar with Alzheimer's and other dementias. The sisters decided to make a doctor's appointment for their mother.

Abigail took time off work to come back from Dayton to go with Mary and Nancy. After three hours of testing by a neurologist and a sociologist, the diagnosis was early dementia, probably Alzheimer's. A prescription was given to hopefully slow the progression of the disease. A social worker discussed help options available for Mary. The sisters decided to hire Mary's next-door neighbor, Karen Nettle, to look after their mother every morning and evening.

Karen would help Mary dress and eat a good breakfast. Before leaving, Karen would fix her a lunch for later. She would return in the evening with a light supper to be sure Mary ate, took her medicine, and dressed for bed. Nancy would increase her visits to her mother. Abigail would make the four-hour trip home more frequently to help when she could. This system would work out for now, but the doctor warned that as the disease progressed, more care would be needed.

Nancy could go riding more frequently when she met her three women friends who also owned horses and relished riding and horse camping. Harry was supportive of her other opportunities to ride. He realized that Nancy's time on Bright Beauty helped her to fight off looming depression from her father's death and her mother's disease.

Nancy was sixty-six when she met each of the other desperate horse wives.

5 DESPERATE HORSE WIVES

Nancy met Bristol first, before the others. They were both shopping at Walmart and needed to use the restroom at the same time. There were three stalls, one in use. Before either of them could enter their own stall, the woman in the first stall cried out, "Help me! Please help me."

"What?" Nancy was surprised. "What do you need?" The woman sounded more distressed than just from a lack of toilet paper. She looked at Bristol who shrugged and entered her own stall.

"I'm stuck. I need help." The voice behind the door pleaded.

"Well, yes, I'll help you, but what exactly is wrong?" Nancy wondered if she were constipated, but there would be nothing she could do about that.

“I’m stuck to the seat and I can’t get up.” The woman began to cry.

Bristol finished drying her hands and told the woman to unlock the door. When it opened the two women wondered why the other could not get up. She was a normal weight. Was she disabled? There was no walker or other sign of disability.

“Give each of us one of your arms, and we’ll pull you up together,” Nancy suggested.

As they pulled, the woman let out a yell. “Stop! That hurts! I’m really stuck here and it’s pulling my skin. I don’t know what to do.” She resumed her crying. “I’m so embarrassed.”

“How could she be stuck?” Nancy wondered aloud, looking at Bristol. “I think this is a problem beyond us. I’ll go for help if you’ll stay with her.”

“Yeah, sure.” Nancy left the restroom and Bristol asked the woman her name.

“Lucy. Thank you for staying with me. I’m so scared and so mortified.”

“I’m Bristol. Let me wrap my rain jacket around you a bit to cover you up some. The help coming might be male, and this will make you feel less exposed.”

The idea of being seen this way by men made Lucy cry more and her cheeks turn red.

Nancy came in with two men in tow. They did not seem embarrassed as they focused on the problem. Lucy covered her face with her hands the whole time they were there. They left for some tools to take the seat off the toilet.

"See, it will be OK. Help is here. I'll stay with you until the men get you released." Bristol's voice was soothing.

"I'll stay, too. I'm Nancy."

The other two told Nancy their names.

"What brings you out to Walmart on this rainy day, Bristol?" Nancy tried to make normal conversation to distract Lucy while waiting for her release.

"I was going to ride my horse, but it was raining, so I came here for some stuff to take on my horse camping trip next week end."

"Oh, really? I go camping with my horse, too. Where do you go?"

"I like Beaver Creek, Hocking Hills, Zalesky Forest, a couple of places in Pennsylvania. Anywhere they have a horsemen's camp, really. I used to ride with some groups, but that was a while back. How about you?"

"Mostly I go to Beaver Creek, sometimes to Harrison Forest. Have you been to Ray Smith's in PA? He holds good rides and feeds you well."

Before Bristol could answer, the two men returned with tools.

As they worked to remove the toilet seat, a woman with a young girl in tow came into the restroom. She stopped just inside the doorway. "What…?!"

"Small problem," Bristol told her. "I think this restroom's closed for now."

The men continued working. "I called 911," one of them

informed the others. "We're taking the seat off so the paramedics can do something when they get here."

A siren in the distance grew louder as it approached. Before the paramedics arrived, Bristol and Nancy were exchanging phone numbers.

The Walmart employees left when the paramedics arrived. Before trying to detach Lucy from her seat, they took her vitals. Bristol and Nancy had stepped back to give them room to work. When they attempted to lift Lucy away from the seat she screamed in pain. They placed her on the gurney on her stomach with the toilet seat still attached to her back side and covered her with a light blanket and Bristol's rain jacket.

"That's mine." Bristol grabbed it off the gurney as it was going out the door. "Good luck," she called to Lucy.

"Sorry this happened to you," Nancy added. "Geez, I have to pee. I came in here to do that, but …"

"Yeah, I'll give you a call. We can go riding together. Maybe a day ride at Quail Hollow or Walborn Reservoir. Good to meet you. Bye." Bristol hoped it would work out. She was tired of riding alone.

The next day Bristol called Nancy to tell her the eleven o'clock news aired a story about a woman who had been stuck to a toilet seat in a Walmart store restroom. "It must be Lucy. I bet she's really happy they didn't give her name."

"I saw that, too, last night. They said someone put super glue on the seat, and she must have sat down before it dried."

They chatted about general things for a few minutes then made plans to meet at Quail Hollow for a ride. Nancy had her Missouri Fox Trotter mare, Bright Beauty. Bristol was riding her dream horse, a black and white Spotted Saddle Horse she named Hot Stuff. Both horse breeds were smooth gaited and they were well matched in pace. They chatted during a lunch break. The ride was enjoyable for both women, so they made plans to ride together again.

Before they could meet, Bright Beauty gave Nancy and Harry a scare. It was supper and turn out time for Beauty. She had been stalled all afternoon away from the heat of the day and the flies. After finishing her small amount of grain, she would be turned out to graze in the pasture, but she did not eat her grain. She hung her head. Now and then, she turned her head to look back at her stomach as though wondering why it hurt.

Nancy checked the floor of the stall. The hay was gone, but there was no poop. "Oh, Beauty, looks like you have colic. Oh, my girl." Nancy rubbed her horse's neck, then reached for the halter and lead rope hanging outside the stall door. The first thing was to walk the horse. If there was no bowel movement shortly, she would call the vet. Walking the horse with one hand, she used her other hand to call Harry at the house, using her cell phone. "Honey, Bright Beauty has colic. I don't know how bad, but I'm walking her now. Just wanted you to know I won't be back in for a while. Go ahead and eat. Supper's in the crock pot."

Instead of eating his dinner, Harry joined her in the pasture. "Did she poop yet?"

"No, and I'm getting worried. I think I'll call the vet."

"Here. Let me walk her for a bit. I brought you out a lawn chair. Sit down and call the vet."

The vet's office told Nancy it would be at least two hours until the doctor could be at her barn. "Keep walking her, give her nothing to eat, and don't let her roll. Try to keep her on her feet.

Good luck."

Nancy's next call was to Bristol to cancel their planned ride for the next day. Bristol said she understood, and she surprised Nancy by showing up before the vet did.

"I figured you could use the moral support, and I could take a turn walking her. How is she doing?"

"Some better. She passed gas, but she hasn't pooped yet. Thanks for coming. Harry has been taking turns with me to keep her walking, but I sent him to the house for his supper. Did you eat yet?"

Bristol had eaten, and she shooed Nancy to the house for her supper. "I'll walk Beauty 'til you get done and let you know if there are any changes." She took the lead rope and headed down the pasture with the horse.

By the time the vet arrived, Bright Beauty had passed several droppings. The vet gave the horse Banamine, an analgesic pain killer. The poor horse was so miserable she allowed the vet to run a tube down her throat to administer mineral oil directly into her stomach without having to sedate her. Bristol stayed until the vet left and Bright Beauty was feeling better.

"Thank you so much, Bristol. You were so sweet to come. I was worried there for a bit. It was really thoughtful of you."

Nancy's first impressions of Bristol were good ones.

...

Nancy met Lavern in the early fall after riding all spring and summer with Bristol. Lavern and Nancy were in the same aisle of Walmart when they witnessed a man eat a donut without paying for it. He looked comical with powdered sugar all over his face while trying to be furtive. They looked at each other, began to chuckle, then shrugged their shoulders and began to talk. They discovered they both had horses and enjoyed camping and trail riding with them. They planned a few rides together with Bristol when schedules permitted. As they rode, they decided to plan a camping trip before the end of fall.

"We'll go in October to see the fall color," Bristol stated as a matter of fact as though the other two had no say.

They went to Beaver Creek the second weekend of October. Around campfires, Lavern told them about her teaching career that had just begun two months earlier. Nancy shared her fears about her mother's dementia. Bristol expressed her desire to learn to play guitar and accompany herself singing.

Fall color had almost peaked. Reds, rusts, oranges, and yellows mixed with shades of green. The sun shone through the veil of colorful leaves and created shadows on the ground that moved with the breeze. The weather was dry with perfect temperatures, cool mornings and evenings, and warm afternoons. The trails were dry, and the horses were energetic in the crisp fall air.

Bristol had a few snippy moments and Charlie kept calling Lavern on her cell phone. Otherwise, they had a great time.

Nancy had the feeling all was not well with Lavern and Charlie. She invited Lavern on a couple of day rides so just the two of them could talk. Lavern did open up. She told Nancy how Charlie was controlling and not supportive of her horse ownership. She explained about the death of her family, how she struggled the next two years to stay in school and keep her horse. She spoke about her feelings of anger toward God for not protecting her family. Trying to end on a positive note she said, "I guess I should be grateful for Charlie. It was easier after he married me. I just thought married life would be more supportive and less controlling."

"I'll pray for peace and contentment between you and Charlie. Your family, well, I'm just so sorry. The scripture says, now we see as in a mirror darkly, but then, meaning when we're in Heaven, we will see clearly. Do you believe in God's time? Do you remember the verse in Ecclesiastes, or do you know the song with those words, about there is a season for everything under Heaven?"

Lavern nodded.

Nancy continued, "A time to live and a time to die. I'm not saying God planned the accident. I guess I'm saying there are things in this life we don't understand, and everything will come to its fulfillment under God's purpose. I'll pray for your peace and acceptance of your family's death, and that you come back to your connection with God."

The two women hugged.

Bristol found out Nancy rode alone with Lavern without inviting her, and she became jealous. "I thought we were friends!" she blurted.

"Bristol, I do consider you my friend, but it's rather high schoolish of you to feel I shouldn't do things with anyone else unless you're included."

Bristol refused Nancy's calls for a week after that. Nancy prayed Bristol would be healed from whatever insecurities plagued her.

...

Nancy met Elise and Jolene in Walmart late that winter. Mother and daughter were shopping in the feminine products aisle of Walmart. Just as Jolene grabbed a box of Tampons, a small, wiry, gray-haired lady turned down the aisle with a red-headed stock boy. She was elderly, but not frail. She was pulling him along. His face was nearly as red as his hair. Seeing the young, pretty teenager who was about to witness his embarrassment, he tried to pull away from the spry elder, but she held a grip.

Nancy came around the corner to walk down the aisle in time to hear the old woman proclaim in jubilation, "There now, see? This is the section we'll find it in. I never knew about these things when I was young, but it's what my granddaughter uses. She's visiting me from Denver this week and needs some. She'd get them herself, but she doesn't feel well."

She dropped his arm and the stock boy tried to slink away, but grandma grabbed his shirt and tugged him back.

Embarrassed to be seen with it in front of the stock boy, Jolene hid her box of Tampons in their cart under some of Elise's purchases. Jolene wanted to leave the aisle, but Elise whispered, "Wait." She wanted to hear the rest of this play out. Nancy, too, had stopped to hear the rest.

Grandma said to the young man, "I forgot to ask my granddaughter what size I should buy, so I need help picking out the right ones. She's about my height. What size do you think I am?"

The stock boy managed to choke out, "Ma'am, you better ask these ladies." He extricated himself from grandma's grip and fled, mortified.

Nancy and Elise looked at each other and nearly choked holding back their laughter. Jolene's embarrassment subsided and she began to see the humor in the situation. Elise told the grandmother tampons did not come sized for body type and helped her pick out a brand for her granddaughter. "My daughter likes these for comfort," Elise suggested.

When grandma was out of earshot, Nancy, Elise, and Jolene were still standing there. Nancy and Elise looked at each other and let out the laughter they were holding in. They began to talk. The subject of horses quickly arose.

"What do you do with yours?" Jolene always asked when she met another horse owner.

Nancy always enjoyed talking about horses. "I like to trail ride. I do some day rides around here, but my favorite thing is to go camping and ride through the woods from morning until late afternoon. How about you?"

"That's what Mom and I do, too! Have you ever been to West Branch or Quail Hollow for day rides? Do you go camping at Beaver Creek?"

"Yes, all the time. What breed do you have?"

"Tricked Out and Tucker are Tennessee Walkers," Elise answered.

"Bright Beauty is a Missouri Fox Trotter mare."

The three women began to slowly walk down the aisle as they continued to talk.

"I have two other friends I ride with. You'd be welcome to

join us," Nancy invited. They ended up exchanging names and telephone numbers and agreeing to plan a day ride together.

...

Nancy arranged for everyone to meet at a local restaurant in Ravenna on the first Saturday in March. She introduced everyone to Bristol as they came in. The women seemed to be compatible and they decided to try to ride together.

Toward the end of March, the weather turned warm enough for a day ride together. Nancy telephoned each of the others to set the time and place. They met at the parking lot for the trail head in Brecksville Metro Park. The bridle paths there were well maintained and groomed to drain water. Normally there was little or no mud, so it was a safe bet that the trails would be dry enough.

The horses were eager to be back on trail after a winter break, and they were excited to meet other horses, but they were well-mannered. With a lot of snorting, they moved off briskly in the crisp, early spring air that smelled of the musky, damp earth and new green life. There was no mud, and there were no bugs. The leaves on the deciduous trees were not yet out, but the woods had a seasonal beauty with many shades of tender green, darker evergreen conifers, evergreen Christmas fern, blue and purple bird foot violets, the tiny yellow flowers of the fragrant sumac, the bright blue to pink flowers of the sharp lobe hepatica, the nodding bright yellow flowers of the yellow trout-lily, and the star-shaped blue, pink, and white of the spring beauty flowers. They saw finches, grouse, and cardinals feeding on the pussy willows. Lavern pointed to the showy white flowers of the bloodroot, but none of the women realized they were fortunate to see them. The flowers of the bloodroot last only a few days, and their entire flowering season lasts only one or two weeks.

Everyone enjoyed the ride and enjoyed each other. They decided to meet for Equine Affaire which was again held the second weekend in April. Bristol drove by herself for the shopping on Saturday. Nancy, Lavern, Elise, and Jolene traveled to Columbus together for the weekend. Bristol met them for the Fantasia show on Saturday night. The women proved to be companionable and began planning horse camping trail rides.

By May, the four desperate horse wives had begun horse camping and riding together on monthly trips. They encouraged and supported each other, consoled each other, and celebrated each other. Each of the husbands reacted differently as their wives headed out.

Harry bid Nancy to be safe and have fun.

Ric hoped Bristol would return in a better mood.

Charlie whined and complained that Lavern was leaving him home alone for the weekend.

Marty could care less whether Elise and Jolene went away or not.

The wives each needed the trips to relax, unwind, and for a few short weekends, escape their desperate lives. It was a time to regroup, recharge, and relax. They each considered that no one had a perfect life, and their lives riding their horses in the beauty of nature made the rough times bearable.

…

Desperate Horse Wives, available from Amazon in paper back and on Kindle, continues to unfold the poignant and emotional stories of the four main characters in Becoming

Desperate. There are adventures on the horse trails, family difficulties, misplaced romance, betrayals, and revenge. Read it for a wild ride through rocky woodlands and through their rockier relationships as they face their fears of life's challenges.

Following is an excerpt from Desperate Horse Wives:

The riders lined up at the crossing. The water was high and swift, very dark, and maybe three feet deep. Even Jolene had second thoughts about crossing until Bristol pushed past her on Hot Stuff, causing Tricked Out to move over a step. Hot Stuff brushed against Jolene's knee as Bristol challenged, "Come on you dudes. You can do this."

Hot Stuff hesitated to enter the river, so Bristol jabbed him with her spurs. He entered the water. One by one, the other horses followed.

Nancy called a warning to the others. "Don't look down at the water. You'll get dizzy. Look across to the shore."

"Slow Trick down," Elise yelled to Jolene. "The rocks are slippery, and the current's strong."

Jolene slowed her horse so he could carefully place one hoof at a time across the rocks. As they reached the center of the swollen river, Trick slipped and fell sideways, throwing Jolene out of the saddle on the downstream side. After hitting her head on a rock, the current carried her away from under the horse, a split second before Trick landed on his side, saving her from being crushed. Her flailing hands grabbed the stirrup, keeping her from floating down the river. Holding tight to the stirrup with her left hand, she reached higher with her right hand to grab the saddle horn and lift herself higher from the water. Trick struggled to stand against the current. Jolene lost her grip on the saddle horn.

Happy Trails To You,
Janet

JanetRFoxAuthor@mail.com
On Facebook as Janet R Fox Author

Made in the USA
Middletown, DE
10 November 2017